Neil Duffield

Neil has written more than fifty plays and adaptations which have been staged extensively throughout Britain and abroad. In 2006, he won the Arts Council England Children's Award 'for work which displays excellence, inspiration and innovation in children's theatre.'

Recent work includes *Dancing in my Dreams* (Oxfordshire Theatre Company); *A Christmas Carol* (Octagon Theatre, Bolton); *Leopard* (Crucible Theatre, Sheffield); *The Hunchback of Notre Dame* and *The Lost Warrior* (Dukes Theatre, Lancaster); *The Snow Queen, The Jungle Book* and *Arabian Nights* (Watermill Theatre, Newbury); *The Firebird* (Northumberland Theatre Company); and *The Secret Garden* (Helix Theatre, Dublin).

He lives in Bolton with his wife, theatre director Eileen Murphy.

Also published by Aurora Metro Press

A Christmas Carol by Charles Dickens

adapted for the stage by Neil Duffield

ISBN 978-09551566-8-7

£8.99

For more good books and plays:

www.aurorametro.com

PLAYS FOR YOUTH THEATRES AND LARGE CASTS

written and introduced by

NEIL DUFFIELD

with a preface by
Karen Simpson

AURORA METRO PRESS

This volume first published in Great Britain 2009 by Aurora Metro Publications Ltd, 67 Grove Avenue, Twickenham, TW1 4HX www.aurorametro.com
© Aurora Metro Publications Ltd. 2009 info@aurorametro.com

Cover image: istockphoto.com/solarseven © James Thew 2007

Editor: Cheryl Robson

With thanks to: Aidan Jenkins, Neil Gregory, Gabriele Maurer, Simon Bennett, Cordelia Makartsev, Carmel Walsh.

Introduction and plays © Neil Duffield 2009

Preface © Karen Simpson 2009

Printed in the UK by CPI Antony Rowe Chippenham and Eastbourne

ISBN 978 -1- 9065820-6-7

Preface

Neil Duffield's plays have delighted and enthralled audiences of all ages, the length and breadth of the UK for many years now. In schools, community centres, arts centres and theatres, his plays have formed a pivotal part in introducing theatre to new audiences. Greek Gods, African myths and legends, fairy tales, characters from history, characters from the here and now, all live side by side in his work. He writes plays that can be performed by one actress and plays that encompass a whole community, whether fantasy or reality, all are treated with the same integrity and passion.

I first experienced his work as an audience member – a mum along with her three small daughters – about twenty years ago. Not long afterwards, I found myself nervously approaching him as a very inexperienced young director. In directing my first play of his, I started to discover what makes Neil's work so very special. He is a master of story-telling, able to craft stories into dramatic form, so that audiences are, quite simply, taken on a journey. As a director, I trusted his stage directions and dialogue and soon realised that I really couldn't go wrong.

Since that first venture, I have had the very good fortune to work alongside Neil on many productions. This new collection of his plays is an opportunity for other people to enjoy and learn from his work.

Karen Simpson
Artistic Director, Oxfordshire Theatre Company

CONTENTS

Introduction

The four plays in this collection are aimed principally at the 12-16 age range and intended for large cast youth theatre and school productions. However, the plays are equally suitable for mixed groups of both adults and young people staging plays in an amateur or community drama group. There is also some leeway at either end of the age range. **Small Fry** has been performed by 10-11 year olds, while the other three have all been produced by groups made up of older teens and those in their early twenties.

None of the plays involve demanding requirements in terms of set, props or costume. These can be as simple or as elaborate as desired. All, to some extent, require music or percussion but this can be either live or recorded depending on resources, and there are no songs. Movement work features strongly, and all four are dramatic adventure stories.

Twice upon a Time is the most recent play in the collection and was written specifically for a large cast youth theatre production. It was commissioned by Dundee Rep and at the time of writing is still in rehearsal. My brief was either to write a full-length play in which Act 1 and Act 2 would have different casts, or two shorter plays which are linked in some way. Never having attempted it before, I opted to write a play which could be performed by two different groups.

Twice Upon A Time rehearsal

At Dundee Rep, the youth theatre has divided its members into two

groups of 24 young people, one group of 14-16 year-olds and the other comprising 16-18 year-olds. In a very real sense it's been a theatrical experiment. The process has been organic with a strong input from the young people themselves. Working with them and with Sarah Brigham and Gemma Nicol (their two directors) has been a positive joy.

Twice Upon A Time rehearsal

Small Fry was written to be performed by classes of school children in York, Plymouth, Dundee and South West London. It was commissioned by Juliet Forster of York Theatre Royal as part of an adventurous but much under-recognised initiative called The Playhouse Project – an annual co-operation between York Theatre Royal, Plymouth Theatre Royal, Dundee Rep and Polka Theatre in Wimbledon. Each year, four writers are commissioned to write a play to be performed by young people in all four cities. The highlight, of course, is the festival itself,

Small Fry performance

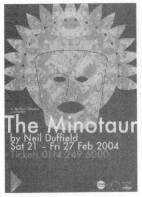

involving hundreds of children and young people performing on the stages of some of the country's most prominent theatres. But before that takes place, writers, directors and teachers from all the participating cities are invited to spend a weekend together in Cornwall working on and developing the scripts. For everyone involved it's an invaluable experience. I'm hoping one day they'll invite me to do it again!

The Minotaur was also originally written for a small professional cast and commissioned by The Crucible Theatre, Sheffield. Karen Simpson, who at the time was Education Director, is someone I've worked with many times over the years. Together we held workshops in a number of Sheffield schools to explore various themes and ideas. What became apparent among the young people with whom we worked, was a strong interest in myth and legend. Having explored a few alternatives, we eventually agreed to base the play on the Greek myth of Theseus and the Minotaur.

Photo: Chris Saunders Sheffield Crucible's *The Minotaur.*

Talking With Angels performed by Quicksilver Theatre

Talking With Angels is based on the story of Joan of Arc. It was originally commissioned by Quicksilver Theatre Company in London and performed on tour by a company of four professional actors. After receiving a number of requests from youth theatres and educational establishments, I later reworked it for larger casts. It has been performed quite extensively by youth theatre, school, college and university groups both in Britian and the USA.

None of these plays would have been written without the help and support of the directors who commissioned them – Karen Simpson (now at Oxfordshire Theatre Company), Juliet Forster at York Theatre Royal, Guy Holland at Quicksilver, and Sarah Brigham and Gemma Nicol at Dundee Rep.

To all of them my deepest thanks. Also, and just as importantly, to my partner, Eileen Murphy, who acts as inspiration and mentor on all my work.

Neil Duffield

TWICE UPON A TIME

Premiered by Dundee Rep Youth Theatre Company July 2009

Suzanne Arnot – **Logan**

Kate Adams – **Demon**

Rachel Anderton – **Zita**

Hayleigh Cameron – **Yelena**

Nicola Chalmers – **Carman**

Ellie Crabb – **Assistant Director**

Marley Davidson – **Demon**

Lewis Davie – **Demon**

Alex Dolan – **Callum**

Stacy Duffy – **The Callieach**

Ella Duncan – **Lucca**

Cally Evans – **Demon**

Sarah Farrell – **Demon**

Sophie Gilbert – **Darla**

Syan Gilroy-Milne – **Carman**

Georgia Gray – **Rolo**

Christine Haggart – **Freya**

Jeff Hannan – **Demon/Design**

Chris. Harrison – **Family**

Daniel Hird – **Assistant Director**

Morgan Hutchison – **Freya**

Steven Lafferty – **Family**

Gabriella Laverty – **Family**

Andrew Manzi – **Callum**

Rachael McArthur – **Demon**

Laura McIntosh – **Darla**

Kieran Menzies – **Demon/Design**

Kirsten Millar – **Family/Design**

Steven Moyes – **Magus**

Liam Muir – **Family**

Aislin Mullholland – **Demon**

Rachel Murray – **Assistant Director**

Maisie Peebles – **Lucca**

Amy Quinn – **Zita**

Callum Ramage – **Logan/Composer**

Emily Schofield – **Family**

Scott Smith – **Demon**

Brett Stewart – **Demon**

Alice Sturrock – **The Callieach**

Jasmine Summerton – **Drake**

Joe Summerton – **Rolo**

Jordan Thomson – **Magus**

Roy Thomson – **Family**

Lizzie Watson – **Family/Design**

Rebecca Watson – **Drake**

Naomi Weir – **Yelena**

Charlotte Wells –**Assistant Stage Manager**

NOTE: Lizzie Watson, Chris Harrison and Jeff Hanan will be in both acts.

TWICE UPON A TIME

Twice Upon A Time

The themes for this play came from the young people it was written for. They emerged from a day-long workshop held at Dundee Rep, led by Sarah Brigham and Gemma Nicol which involved a carefully structured series of improvisations.

At the end of the day, the young people (about 40 of them, aged 14-18) were asked to write down what they would most like the play to be about. What came out was the following list (more or less in order of popularity):

Magic
The nature of time
Adventure
Time travel
Love
Fear of the unknown
Loss of self
Relationship between fantasy and reality
Inner demons
Gay relationships

I kept this list in front of me as the play developed, determined to try and fit as much of it as I could into the jigsaw. But what began to emerge for me was an interlinking theme concerning different worlds and the borders between them. Another list began to take shape, a list of different worlds:

Worlds separated by geography and culture
The world of dreams
Internal worlds/ The world in our heads.
Virtual worlds/ The world of video games and the internet
Worlds separated by time.
The world of memory lost./ A world with no past
Supernatural worlds

Crossing the borders between these worlds is sometimes impossible, sometimes very easy, and all of us cross them, or at least think of crossing them, at some point in our lives. The borders are not always obvious. Sometimes we find ourselves inhabiting several worlds at once. And sometimes we become exiles – cut off from the world we know best.

TWICE UPON A TIME

Commissioned by Dundee Repertory Theatre's Youth Theatre and first performed on July 7th, 2009.

Directed by Sarah Brigham & Gemma Nicol; Designed by Leila Kalbassi; Composer Ivan Stott; Costume Designer Phyllis Byrne; Lighting Designer Emma Jones; Young Person Assistant Directors Daniel Hird & Rachel Murray; DSM on the book Elaine Diffenthal; Youth Theatre Assistants Hannah Davies and Bonnie Smith.

CHARACTERS

Some of the characters are played by two actors. If desired, the whole play can be performed by two separate casts – one for each act.

Magus (m) – the Storyteller
Yelena (f) – a young woman
Callum (m) – a young man
The Cailleach (f) – mythological Celtic witch queen
Demons (both male and female, as many as required)

Callum's companions:
Lucca (f)
Logan (m)
Drake (m)
Darla (f)
Rolo (m)

Freya (f) – goddess of beauty, goddess of perfection
Family – Yelena's imaginary family (male and female, as many as required)
Zita (f) – Yelena's sister
Carmen (f) – Zita's lover

ACT ONE

Music, mysterious and magical, underscores the whole of the opening sequence which should have a dream-like quality throughout.

Light fades up on Magus. His costume is timeless and of a somewhat eccentric nature denoting his role as a storyteller. He holds a video games disc (DVD).

Behind him, in the background, we see a moving projection of rainbow lights, representing as near as possible the iridescent reflections on the surface of the games disc. The projection continues throughout the opening sequence.

Magus   In a time beyond time
                   In a land beyond land

Magus aims the disc at an area of the stage almost as if directing a beam of light.

Magus   Enter the circle of rainbow light.

He draws Yelena onto the stage. She is a young woman dressed in roughly made clothing, a mixture of past and present with hints of a foreign culture. She looks around as if hoping to meet someone. Magus aims the disc in a different direction.

Magus   Enter the land where time stands still.

He draws Callum onto the stage. A young man dressed in similar fashion to Yelena but without the hints of foreign culture. They are lovers, meeting together after not seeing each other for some time. Overjoyed, they move towards one another. Hold hands. Embrace. Celebrate their re-union. Neither has any awareness of Magus's presence. Magus aims the disc in another direction.

Magus   Enter the realm of memory lost.

He draws a throng of Demons onto the stage. Half-masked and with stylized movement. They watch Callum and Yelena closely but show no awareness of Magus. Magus aims the disc in yet another direction.

Magus   Enter the world of dreams.

He draws the Cailleach onto the stage. A blue-faced witch queen. Half-masked and of nightmarish appearance. Magus and the Cailleach stare straight at each other. She is the only one who displays any awareness of his presence and regards him as a challenge to her power.

A momentary image of the two lovers and the opposing forces of the Cailleach and Magus. Magus lowers the disc and the Cailleach immediately directs the Demons towards Callum and Yelena. The two lovers are about to kiss but the Demons attract Callum's attention and prevent it.

All the following dialogue is addressed to Callum.

Demon   Come.

Demon   Follow me.

Demon   Follow me.

Demon   Follow me over.

The Demons manage to come between Callum and Yelena and separate them.

Demons   Follow me to the Otherworld.

Callum and Yelena try to come together again but the Demons prevent it.

Demon   Come.

Demon   Follow me.

Demon	Follow me.
Demon	Follow me over.
Demons	Follow me to the Otherworld.

(They attempt to entice Callum away.)

Demon	A chieftain's crown upon your head.
Demon	A horse that rides the wind.
Demon	The sweetest music will fill your ears.
Demon	The fairest of beauties will dance as your bride.

Under the Cailleach's direction and with Callum distracted, other Demons start to drag Yelena away. Still to Callum:

Demon	Enter the circle of rainbow light.
Demons	Follow me to the Otherworld.
Demon	Enter the land where time stands still.
Demons	Follow me to the Otherworld.
Demon	Enter the realm of memory lost.
Demons	Follow me to the Otherworld.

Yelena makes one last desperate attempt to reach Callum but his attention is on the Demons and he doesn't notice as they drag her off stage. The Cailleach appears before him. Callum tries to back away but the Demons prevent him.

The Cailleach	Look into my eyes. (*He doesn't look.*) Are you afraid? Look into my eyes. (*He looks. *)
Demon	She is the circle of rainbow light.
Demon	She is the face in your dreams.
Demon	She is the mist that clouds your thought.

Demon	She is the worm in your mind.
Demon	She is the vision that blurs your sight.
Demon	She is the end of time.
Demon	She is the dark of memory lost.
Demons	She is the Cailleach.
Demons	Cailleach Bheur.

She offers him her hand. He takes it. The Cailleach and Demons lead Callum off.

Magus   In a time beyond time.
                In a land beyond land.

Lights down. Magus exits. Music and projection fade out. The dream sequence ends.

Lights up. We are in the far distant future. Outdoor location. Yelena enters, dressed as we saw her in the opening sequence. She carries a small sack and a game snare and moves with caution.

Callum *(from off)* Who is it? Who goes there! *(Yelena searches round for an escape route. She can't decide which way to go.)*
     (from a different direction) Speak! ...Who are you? Declare yourself!

Yelena makes a run for it. Straight into Callum. He too is as we saw him in the opening sequence, but now carries a stout wooden staff as a weapon and clearly knows how to use it. There is a brief struggle. He overpowers her. Corners her with the staff.

Callum   What have you got there? ... Hand it over.

She gives him the snare. He examines it briefly, tosses it aside, motions to the sack.

Yelena   It's nothing. Only a rabbit.

He takes the sack from her. Opens it. Glances inside.

Callum   What is it with you exiles? Why do you come
here? This is our land. (*She doesn't respond, but stares hard at him.*) What are you looking at? Why are you staring?
(*He looks at her more closely.*)
I know you, don't I? I've met you before.

Yelena   And I you.

Callum   Where? Where have I seen you?

Yelena   Somewhere ... I don't know.

Callum   Where are you from?

Yelena   Far away.

Callum   You can't stay. Any of you. Not here. There's
nothing for you.

Yelena   ... In my dreams.

Callum   What?

Yelena   Where we met. You were in my dreams.

Callum (*uneasy*)   I'm here to stop people like you. Keep exiles out.

Yelena   Callum

Callum   You know my name?

Yelena   We were ... (*She pauses, hesitates to say the
word*)

Callum   What?... What were we?

Yelena   Lovers?

Callum   Lovers?

Yelena   You and I. We were lovers.

Callum   Are you mad? ... Who are you? Why have you come here?

Yelena   You remember it, don't you? You've had the same dreams. I can see it in your eyes.

Callum   You've no right to be here. These are the lands of the clan. You have to leave. Now. Straight away.

Yelena   Lights ... In the dreams, Callum. Don't you remember? There were rainbow lights.

Callum   I don't know what you're talking about.

Yelena   Yes, you do. I know you do. It was here ... This place ... But not the same. It was different somehow.

Callum   This is crazy talk. How did you get here? Where are you living?

Yelena   In the woods. With my sister. We have a shelter.

Lucca (calling from off) Callum!

Callum (urgent)   Take the rabbit. It's yours. Now go.

Yelena   Will I see you again?

Callum   I'm a warrior of the clan.

Yelena   Tomorrow.

Callum   Don't you understand? I guard the border. It's not safe for you here. You could be killed.

She smiles, kisses him.

Drake (calling from off) Callum, are you there!

Yelena   Here. At dawn.

She's moves to exit.

Callum   Wait. (*She stops.*) What's your name?

Yelena   Don't you remember?

Callum   ... Yelena.

Logan (*calling from off*) Callum!

Darla (*calling from off*) Callum, are you there?

Yelena   Dawn. Tomorrow.

She exits. Rolo enters, sees Callum.

Rolo   Here! I've found him! Over here! He's here!

The rest of Callum's companions enter. Lucca, Darla, Logan, Drake and Magus. All are dressed in similar fashion to Callum, except Magus who is as we saw him in the opening sequence.

Lucca, Logan, Drake, Darla and Rolo hastily form a line. Magus stays to one side.

Callum   What's all this about?

When they're ready, they speak.

Lucca   We are the bearers of momentous news.

Logan   News of the utmost magnitude.

Drake   And tremendous portent.

Darla   Not to say of immense import.

Rolo   And very important.

Lucca   News of an earth-shattering nature.

Logan   Unprecedented.

Drake   Unbelievable and unforeseen.

Darla	Not to say of unparalleled unpredictability.
Rolo	And very unusual.
Lucca	News of paramount significance.
Logan	Of the most far-reaching consequence.
Drake	Of fundamental relevance.
Darla	Not to say of supreme pertinence.
Rolo	And very...

Callum *(interrupting)* Just get on with it, will you.

Rolo is put out. Lucca takes a breath.

Lucca	A discovery has been made.
Logan	By my good self.
Drake	No.
Darla	I discovered it.
Drake	No you didn't.
Lucca the discoverer.	There can be no dispute about the identity of
Darla	Excuse me.
Lucca I hope?	You're not trying to claim it was you,
Logan	I dug the hole!
Drake	In my patch of earth!
Darla	It was me picked it out.
Lucca	And threw it away!
Logan hadn't seen it stick....	It would have still been under the ground if I

Darla *(interrupting)* I saw it first.

Drake   It doesn't matter who saw it first.

Lucca   Not a one of you recognised its importance.

Logan   The only thing that matters is who discov

Callum *(interrupting)* I don't care who discovered it!

Rolo *(wistful)* It wasn't me. I wasn't even there.

Callum   If you've got something to say, just say it.

Lucca clears her throat.

Lucca   An artifact has been unearthed.

Logan   An historical relic.

Drake   Ancient and antiquated.

Darla   Not to say of an archeological nature.

Rolo   ... It's very old.

Lucca   From before the great climate change.

Logan   Before the burning of the forests.

Drake   And the melting of the ice-caps.

Darla   Not to say the raising of the oceans.

Rolo   ... Very very old.

Lucca   From before the global famine.

Logan   Before the mass migrations.

Drake   And the wars of hunger.

Darla   Not to say the collapse of civilisation.

Rolo   ... Very very very o −

Callum *(interrupting)* I'd be grateful if one of you would get to
   the point.

Rolo   ... We've found something.

Callum   That much I gathered... So? What is it? Tell me.
(*Lucca opens her mouth to speak..)* No!... Don't tell me.
Is it here? Do you have it with you?

*They all look to Rolo. He produces a games disc. Holds it up for
Callum to see.*

Callum   What is it?

Lucca   Ah ...

Logan   That's where a degree of uncertainty arises.

Drake   A measure of equivocation.

Darla   Not to say ambiguity and ambivalence.

Rolo   We don't know.

Lucca   Most of us think it's some sort of ritualistic
talisman.

Logan   Employed by the ancients in demonic
ceremonies.

Drake   An instrument of the occult.

Darla   Not to say a cabbalistic fetish.

Rolo   A magic mirror.

Lucca   But not Magus.

Logan   He disputes and contests this.

Drake   Differs and diverges from it.

Darla   Not to say stands in opposition.

Rolo   He doesn't agree.

Callum   So what does Magus think it is?

Lucca   The Storyteller is of the opinion it's some sort of
portal.

Logan   Technological interface.

Drake   A conduit.

Darla   Not to say cybernetic route.

Rolo   A pathway.

Callum   Pathway?

Lucca   To the supernatural and paranormal.

Logan   A world of witch queens and demons.

Drake   Goddesses of Beauty and Desire.

Darla   Not to say a land where time stands still.

Rolo   The Otherworld.

Callum   Nothing much out of the ordinary then.
    ... So why bring it to me?

Lucca   You're a warrior of the clan.

Logan   You guard the border.

Drake   Who else better to act as its defender and
    protector?

Darla   Not to say safe keeper and sentinel.

Rolo   We'd like you to guard it for us.

Lucca takes the games disc from Rolo.

Lucca   Can't risk exiles getting their hands on it.

Lucca solemnly hands over the disc to Callum.

Lucca   The future of the clan lies in your hands.

Lucca, Darla, Drake, Logan and Rolo all exit. Magus remains.

Callum   Pathway to the Otherworld?

Magus   I sense you're not convinced.

Callum   You're a good Storyteller, Magus.

Magus   Perhaps it has a story of its own.

Callum   And a voice to tell it with I wouldn't doubt.

Callum turns the disc in the light. Gazes into it. Notices the reflections on its surface.

Callum *(disquieted)*   Rainbow lights.......

Magus   Iridescence.

Callum   What?

Magus   Light split into its component parts. I gather
   you've seen it before ... Perhaps you can remember where.

Callum   You don't believe all that Otherworld stuff?
   Witch queens and demons? Goddesses of Beauty and Desire?

Magus   Superstition is it?

Callum   Magic. Religion. Call it what you will. The only
   thing I trust is my own wits. And the strength of my right arm.

Magus   To guard the border.

Callum   ... What are you after, Magus?

Magus   Curiosity, that's all ... Keeping an eye out for the
   unusual and out-of-place. Like this, for instance.

He picks up Yelena's snare, turns it over in his hands.

Magus   I've known snares like this to be used by exiles.
   Squirrels. Rabbits. Whatever they can catch. I understand one or
   two of them have been seen around here. In the woods. I don't
   suppose you've noticed anything?

Callum   Squirrels or exiles?

Magus   A young woman among them I understand.

Callum   You seem to understand an awful lot.

Magus   There are worse things happen in the world
than falling in love with an exile, Callum.

Callum *(shaken)*   You know?

Magus   Don't worry. Your secret is safe.

Pause. Callum decides to risk confiding in him.

Callum   What do you know about ... *(hesitates)*

Magus   What?

Callum   What do you know about dreams?

Magus   Dreams?

Callum   Can people meet in their dreams? Is that
possible?

Magus   Anything is possible in dreams.

Callum   But what if they really meet? First in their
dreams. And then actually. In real life?

Magus   Dreams are never separate from life. There's
always a connection.

Callum   But there's a difference.

Magus   Sometimes dreams seem like reality. And reality
like dreams. It's a brave man who'd attempt to guard that border.

Callum   And love?

Magus   So you *are* in love?

Callum   Alright. Have your laugh.

Magus   There's no border between dreams and love, any
fool knows that. Although maybe not you.

Callum   You're really enjoying this, aren't you?

Magus   Why try to hide it? It doesn't happen to
everyone, you know. Allow yourself to dream. But tread carefully.

Love's not the only thing dreams are made of.

Callum What's that supposed to mean?

Magus *(indicating the disc)* I'd take good care of that if I were you.

Callum This?

Magus It could contain more than you think.

Callum Pathways to the Otherworld?

Magus You might find yourself surprised.

Magus exits. Callum studies the disc, moving it in the light.

Music in. Projection of rainbow lights. After a few moments the Demons start to appear. Callum immediately drops the disc and grabs his staff ready to defend against them.

Demon She is the circle of rainbow light.

Demon She is the face in your dreams.

Demon She is the mist that clouds your thought.

Demon She is the worm in your mind.

Demon She is the vision that blurs yours sight.

Demon She is the end of time.

Demon She is the dark of memory lost.

Demons She is the Cailleach.

Demons Cailleach Bheur.

Music and projection fade out as Freya appears, a young woman, beautifully and richly attired in a timeless costume. No half-mask.

Callum *(on guard)* Who are you? ... Speak. Declare yourself!

Freya	My name is Freya.
Demon	Goddess of Beauty.
Demon	Goddess of Desire.
Demon	The face in your dreams.
Freya	I have watched you many times, Callum.
Callum	You know my name?
Freya	I am here to declare my love for you.

Callum   What is this? What's going on? Are you some kind of apparition?

Freya   I am come to you from the Otherworld. I wish you to accompany me there.

Demon	Follow me.
Demon	Follow me.
Demon	Follow me over.
Callum	I'm dreaming, aren't I? This isn't real.
Freya	Is my appearance not pleasing to you?
Callum	I don't know you. I've never seen you before.
Freya	Come with me.
Demon	Enter the circle of rainbow light.
Freya	Come.
Demon	Enter the world of dreams.
Freya	Come with me to the Otherworld.
Callum	There's no such place.
Freya	Look into my eyes.
Demons	Look.

Callum holds back. Music in. Haunting. Hypnotic.

Freya   Are you afraid? Warrior of the clan? Look. Look
  into my eyes.

He looks. Starts to fall under her spell.

Freya   Tell me what you see.

Callum   Rainbow lights ...

Demons *(sotto voce)* She is the circle of rainbow light.

Freya   And what do you hear?

Callum   Music ...

Demons *(sotto voce)* She is the mist that clouds your thought.

Freya   Come.

Demon   Follow me.

Demon   Follow me.

Demon   Follow me over.

Freya   Come with me to the Otherworld.

Callum   There is no Otherworld. It doesn't exist.

Demon   A chieftain's crown upon your head.

Demon   A horse that rides the wind.

Demon   The sweetest music will fill your ears.

Callum   It's all superstition. Worlds like that exist only
  in the tales of old men.

Freya   Judge for yourself. Come for one day.

Demons   One day.

She holds out her hand to him.

Freya   Come.

Demon	See what no member of your clan has ever seen.
Demon	And return to tell the tale.
Callum	... One day?
Freya	At dawn tomorrow you will be here, as you are now, guarding the borders of the clan.
Demon	Your name famed throughout the land.
Demon	Your deeds spoken of for generations to come.
Freya	What have you to lose?
Demon	Have you no curiosity?
Demon	No spirit of adventure?
Demon	No sense of daring?
Demon	Warrior of the clan?
Callum	I'd be back here by dawn? ... You swear?

He hesitates a moment longer. Then reaches for her hand. She quickly withdraws it.

Freya	Vow to me that you will stay in the Otherworld till dawn tomorrow.
Demon	Dawn.
Demon	Tomorrow.
Callum	You have my word. As a warrior of the clan.

She takes his hand.
Music. Powerful and magical. Projection of rainbow lights as she invokes a spell.

Freya	Come yarrow come rue
Demons	Bladderwrack and feverfew

Freya	Come scullcap come squill
Demons	Witchhazel and dill
Freya	Come hyssop come hops
Demons	Snake root and moss
Freya	Come spell of demon
Demons	And devil's eye
Freya	And carry this soul to another time!

They all exit. Callum's staff and the games disc are left behind on stage. Music and projection fades out. Lights down. Passage of time. Lights up. The following morning at dawn. Yelena enters cautiously.

Yelena   Callum … Callum, are you there? …
    (*Searches around for him, notices the abandoned staff.*)
    Callum … (*She finds the games disc, picks it up.*)
    Callum … Callum, where are you?

Her imaginary Family begin to appear. They are half-masked and with stylized movement, but very different appearance to the Demons. Sensitive and non-threatening. (NB For speeches, 'Family' denotes one member of the group).

Family (*sotto voce*)   Yelena.

Yelena is apprehensive.

Family	Yelena.
Family	Yelena.
Yelena	Who are you?
Family	Don't you know?
Family	Have you forgotten us?

Yelena   Forgotten?

Family   Don't be afraid.

Family   We are here to help you.

Family *(all)*   We are your family.

Yelena   My family?

Family   Don't you remember?

Yelena   I've never seen any of you before.

Family *(all)*   We are your Family.

Yelena   I have no family – only Zita. Who are you?
Where have you come from?

Family   It's alright.

Family   We won't harm you.

Family   We are here to care for you.

Family   To keep you safe.

Family   As we did when you were a child.

Family *(all)*   We are your Family.

Yelena   You're in my head, aren't you. That's where you
are – in my head. I'm imagining things!

Family   Trust us.

Family   Believe in us.

Family   We have come to help you.

Family   We are on your side.

Yelena   I'm not listening to you! Go away! I'm not
listening!

Family *(all)*   We are your Family.

Yelena   I'm going mad. I'm losing my mind!

She throws the disc down.

Family	Don't be frightened.
Family	We are here to look after you.
Family	Just as we used to do.
Family	All those years ago.
Family	Pick up the disc.
Family	It won't harm you.
Family	Pick it up.
Family	Pick up the disc.

Pause. They wait quietly for her to pick up the disc. Eventually she does so.

Family	It will help you to find him.
Yelena	Callum? ... You know about Callum?
Family	Keep it safe.
Family	It will help you to find him.

The Family start to leave.

Yelena	Where are you going?
Family	Don't be afraid.
Family	We are always here.
Family	Always with you.
Family	You are never alone.
Family *(all)*	We are your family.

Family exit. Yelena is left alone. She studies the disc, wondering about its nature. Zita and Carmen enter warily. Zita is Yelena's older sister.

Carmen is Zita's lover. Both are dressed in similar fashion to Yelena.

Zita   Yelena ...

Yelena quickly hides the disc inside her costume.

Yelena   Zita ...

Zita   Are you alone?

Yelena   Yes.

Carmen *(glancing round)* Are you sure?

Yelena   Of course I'm sure. Who else would there be?

Zita   Did you call us?

Yelena   No.

Zita   You didn't?

Yelena   No.

Carmen   We heard a voice.

Zita   It sounded like you.

Carmen   We were worried. We thought you were in
    trouble.

Yelena   I didn't call.

Zita   Were you talking to someone?

Yelena   Who would I be talking to? There's no one here.
    See for yourselves.

Carmen   You didn't hear anything? Or see anyone?

Yelena   I told you. There's no one here.

Zita   It's not safe to be out on your own, Yelena.
    People have been killed.

Yelena   You don't have to mother me. Either of you. I can take care of myself.

Zita senses Yelena's edginess.

Zita	Something's happened, hasn't it.
Yelena	Nothing's happened.
Zita	What is it? What's wrong?
Yelena	I told you. Nothing!

Zita goes to her.

Zita   Hey ... It's me. Zita. I'm your sister, remember?

Yelena softens a little. Smiles.

Yelena	As if I'm ever allowed to forget.
Zita	I'm not a complete fool either.

Short pause. Yelena decides to share her worries.

Yelena	Where are we from, Zita?
Zita	From?
Yelena	Which part of the world?

Zita and Carmen share a glance.

Zita	You know where we're from.
Yelena	It seems so long ago.
Zita	It is.
Yelena	Will we ever go back?

Zita   Yelena. That life is finished. There's nothing to
go back to.

Carmen   Not for any of us. The land we came from is
dead. There's nothing. No one lives there any more.
No one *can* live there.

Zita   This is our world now. It has to be. There's
nowhere else to go.

Yelena   What about our family?

Zita   We have no family. You know that.

Yelena   Are they *all* dead? Every one? Are none of them
left?

Zita   You were young. Very young. We both were.
There's just the two of us.

Carmen   And me. I'm family too I hope.

Yelena   Were any of our family ... *(hesitates)*

Zita   What?

Yelena   Peculiar.

Zita   Peculiar?

Yelena   You know ... strange ... a bit odd.

Zita   What are you saying?

Yelena   Am I like that? Am I peculiar?

Carmen   Has someone been getting at you? Calling you
names?

Yelena   No one's been getting at me.

Zita   Listen to me, Yelena. You're not peculiar. Or
odd. And if anyone tries to say you are, they'll have me to answer to.
You're perfectly normal. As normal as myself and Carmen. Do you
hear me? Do you understand?

Carmen   What's troubling you, Yelena?... What is it?

Yelena   You'd laugh. You'd say I was stupid.

Zita	No one's going to say you're stupid.

Pause. Yelena decides to take a risk.

Yelena	How do you know you're in love?
Zita	In love?
Yelena	Like you and Carmen. What does it feel like? How can you tell?

Carmen *(laughing)* So that's what it is? That's what's been bothering you. I knew there was something.

Yelena	I said you'd laugh!

Zita Only because we're happy for you. There's nothing peculiar about falling in love, Yelena. It happens all the time – doesn't it, Carmen.

Carmen	Who is it? ...Someone we know?
Zita	A boy or a girl?
Yelena *(hesitant)*	His name is Callum.
Zita	... Callum?

Zita and Carmen share a concerned glance.

Carmen	Callum's a clan name.
Yelena	You think I don't know?
Zita	You're not serious, Yelena? This isn't true?
Yelena	He's a warrior.
Carmen	A warrior?
Yelena	He guards the border.

Zita And you've been meeting with him? When? How often? How many times?

Yelena	Bit of a shaker is it?

Carmen   I don't believe I'm hearing this.

Zita   Yelena, have you any idea of the risk you're taking?.... The clan don't want us here. They think we're trying to take what's theirs. They'll send us away.

Carmen   And that's if we're lucky.

Yelena   You think I'm stupid? You think I don't know that?

Zita   Where did you meet this boy?

Yelena   You really want me to tell you?

Zita   Yes. I really want you to tell me.

Yelena   In my dreams.

Zita   What?

Yelena   We met in our dreams.

Carmen   Oh, so you think it's a joke now, do you?

Yelena   I knew you'd be like this. Both of you.

Zita   Yelena, if this is true it's really dangerous. Not just for you – for me and Carmen, for all of us.

Yelena   Not quite so sure how normal I am now, eh? Think I'm losing my wits, do you?

Carmen   I'm beginning to have my doubts.

Yelena   Well, as it happens, you're right. You're spot on – the pair of you. You want to know what I do? ... I talk to people who aren't there. People in my head. They come to me. They promise to take care of me. They tell me they'll look after me like when I was child. I see them. I hear them. I talk to them. They say they're my family. *(Pause)* So go on, say I'm mad. Say I'm losing my wits. That's what you both think, isn't it! Say it!

Pause. Yelena starts to fall apart.

Zita   Yelena. Listen to me. You're not mad. You're not losing your mind. You have to believe that.

Carmen   Zita's right ... I'm sorry. I shouldn't have said that. It was stupid of me.

Zita   Come with us. Come back to the shelter.

Yelena   No. I have to wait for Callum. He may still come.

Zita   Yelena, it's not safe for you here. People have been killed.

Yelena   You go. Both of you.

Zita   We're not leaving you.

Yelena   Later. I'll come later.

Carmen   Come with us. Come now.

Yelena   I'll be alright ... I won't be long. I promise ... Please.

Zita and Carmen share a look. Decide to leave. Yelena is left alone. After a moment she takes out the disc. Turns it around in her hand. Music in. Projection of rainbow lights. The Cailleach appears.

Yelena   You ... You were there, weren't you ... In the dreams. It was you took him away from me. Who are you?

The Cailleach disappears as music and projection fade out. Magus enters.

Magus   You found it then, I see. (*Startled, Yelena looks for a means of escape.)* It's alright. I won't hurt you. (*She hesitates. He makes no move towards her.)* I'm not a guard. I've not come to drive you out. See ... no weapons. (*She eyes him warily. He indicates the disc)* You've seen the rainbow lights, I presume.

Yelena   I found it. It was lying on the ground.

Magus   I didn't think he'd keep it. Always so sure of himself ... I did try to warn him. You saw the Cailleach also?

Yelena   Her?... Who is she?

Magus   She's many things to many people.

Yelena   What do you mean?

Magus   You're here to meet Callum.

Yelena   You know him?... Where is he? We'd arranged to see each other. Has something happened to him?

Magus   I wouldn't be at all surprised.

Yelena   He's not hurt is he? He's not been....

Magus.   No. Nothing like that ... Gone away in all likelihood.

Yelena   Gone away!

Magus   Perception was never one of Callum's strengths ... You probably don't agree.

Yelena   Gone where? I have to find him. Where is he?

Magus   In the land where time stands still.

Yelena   Why do you talk in riddles?.... Do you know where he is or not?

Magus   He's been taken to the Otherworld.

Yelena   The Otherworld?

Magus   It's a world beyond time. A world where there is only the moment. And the moment lasts for eternity.

Yelena   ... You mean I've lost him? ... I'll never see him again?

Magus   I didn't say that.

Yelena   Then how do I find him? How do I bring him back?

Magus   You have the disc.

Yelena   This?... What is it?

Magus	It's a pathway. A means of crossing the border.
Yelena	Which border?
Magus	The one you choose. Open it.
Yelena	Open it?

Yelena holds up the disc. Stares at it, wondering what to do. Music and projection of rainbow lights. From the direction in which the disc is pointing, Callum appears, as if drawn in by it.
Music and projection fade out.

Yelena	Callum!
Callum	Yelena....

She runs to him. They embrace.

Yelena   I thought I'd lost you. I'd thought I'd never see you again.

Callum   What are you talking about? I've been gone only a short while. But why have you brought me back? We agreed to meet at dawn.

Yelena   Callum, dawn is long gone. Look at the sky.

Callum   Dawn tomorrow. And I'll be here. I promise. But I can't stay. Not now. I have to go back. I gave her my word.

Yelena   Gave *who* your word?

Callum   Her name is Freya. Some sort of ... goddess of beauty ... I don't know. She asked me to go with her.

Yelena   And you went?

Callum   To the Otherworld. I never believed there was such a place. I thought it was all superstition, the stories of old men. But it's real, Yelena – it exists – there is such a world – I've been there. You should see it. Everywhere there are lights – all the colours of the rainbow – dancing and glittering. Winged horses ride through the sky. Palaces of silver tower above the streets. Music and entertainment. Plates piled high. Glasses spilling over. You couldn't begin to imagine such a world.

Yelena   This Freya – are you in love with her?

Callum   I went there out of curiosity. I wanted to know. I wanted to find out if the stories were true.

Yelena   Then stay. Stay here. With me.

Callum   I gave my word. I promised to remain until dawn tomorrow.

Yelena   Callum. This is tomorrow. A whole day's gone by.

Callum   Are you trying to make fun of me? I was here only moments ago – with Magus.

Magus   She's telling you the truth, Callum.

Callum   ...What?

Magus   Time stands still in the Otherworld. There is no tomorrow.

Callum   That's impossible.

Magus   Unimaginable perhaps.

Callum   Is this some kind of joke the two of you are playing?

Yelena   Callum. You have to stay here. You must never go back to that place.

Callum   I gave my word. As a warrior of the clan.

Yelena   And you've kept it. Go back there and you'll stay for ever. We lost each other once before. Don't you remember?

Callum   Those were dreams.

Yelena   More than dreams. You know they were. Don't let it happen again. Stay, Callum. Please. Stay here. With me.

Magus   He cannot.

Yelena   What?

Magus   He has to go back.

Yelena   What are you talking about? Don't listen to him, Callum! Stay. You have to stay!

Magus   He gave his word. As a warrior of the clan. Break it and the demons will return.

Yelena   What demons?

Magus   They won't give him a moment's rest. They'll harass. They'll haunt. They'll torment. They'll never leave him alone until he agrees to go with them. Isn't that so, Callum?

Yelena   Don't listen to him, Callum. Stay here. Please!

Music in. Low and threatening.

Demon *(calling from off)* Liar!

Demon *(calling from off)* Cheat!

Demon *(calling from off)* Backslider!

Callum reacts to each of the voices

Magus   You can hear them now, can't you? They're calling you.

Demon *(calling from off)* Fraudster!

Demon *(calling from off)* Imposter!

Demon *(calling from off)* Double-dealer!

Callum continues to react to the voices.

Yelena   What is it, Callum? What's the matter?

Callum   Don't you hear them?

Magus   These are Callum's demons. Only he can hear
   them.

Demons start to appear – armed with staffs.

Callum   There! You see them? There!

Yelena sees nothing.

Demon   Vow breaker!

Demon   Snake-in-the grass!

Demon   Runaway!

Callum *(pointing out more demons)* And there! ... Look! ... More of
   them!

Yelena sees nothing.

Demon   Yellow-belly!

Demon   Lily-liver!

Demon   Chicken-heart!

*Callum starts to back away. Yelena quickly picks up the staff, offers it
to Callum.*

Yelena   Fight them, Callum. You're a warrior. Fight
   back. Drive them away!

Callum *(taking the staff)* Yes ... Yes. I'll fight them. Demons or no demons. I'll fight them. (*He prepares to fight.*) Come on. I'm not afraid of you. Come on all of you!

Yelena   You mustn't go back. You mustn't let them take you.

Callum   It'll be alright, I promise. Stay over there. Wait for me.

Yelena and Magus move to one side. Demons start to move in on Callum.

Demon   Charlatan!

Demon   Freebooter!

Demon   Judas!

Yelena   Is there no way I can help?

Magus   You have the disc still? (*She takes it from her costume.*) Make sure you guard it well.

Magus moves to a different area of the set where he can oversee what happens without anyone being aware of his presence.
Yelena wonders how best to guard the disc. Finally, she decides to stand on it. Music builds.

Demon   Weakling!

Demon   Faintheart!

Demon   Deserter!

Demon   Coward!

Demons   Sneaking off into the night!

Demon   Runaway!

Demon   Traitor!

Demon	Deceiver!
Demon	Imposter!
Demons	Trying to stay out of sight!

They circle around him, preparing to attack.

Demon	We'll kick you.
Demon	We'll lick you.
Demon	We'll hit you.
Demon	We'll slit you.
Demons	We'll stick you and put out your lights.
Demon	We'll crack you.
Demon	We'll smack you.
Demon	We'll whack you.
Demon	We'll hack you.
Demons	It's a fight, it's a fight, it's a fight!

*Music swells as the battle gets under way. The fight swings this way
and that. Yelena can only look on anxiously, trying to gauge the
progress of the battle as best she can. Finally, Callum manages to
defeat the Demons and drive them away.
Music fades down but still lingers. Yelena sees that Callum has
stopped fighting and relaxed his guard.*

Yelena   Have they gone?... Have you beaten them?

*She moves towards him, leaving the disc unguarded. In a flash a pair
of Demons leap out and grab it.*

Demon	Victory!

Demon *(aiming the disc at Callum)* Enter the realm of memory lost!

Callum immediately renews his guard – this time against Yelena.

Callum	Who is it? Who goes there?
Yelena	Callum, what is it?
Callum	Speak! Who are you?... Declare yourself!
Yelena	What do you mean?... Callum, it's me. Yelena. Don't you recognise me?
Callum	I know you, don't I? I've met you before.
Yelena	Callum, you fought the Demons. You beat them. You're free to stay.
Callum	At dawn tomorrow I shall return to my post. Do not come here again.

The rest of the Demons reappear. Yelena watches helplessly as Callum lays down his staff and moves to join them.

Yelena	Callum ...! No ...! Callum!

She watches as he exits with the demons. At the same time, the two Demons with the disc dash off, but find their exit suddenly blocked by Magus. They stop in their tracks, afraid of his power. He holds out his hand for the disc. They hand it over. Shrink away and exit.

Yelena	Callum! *(suddenly remembering)* The disc ...!

She dashes to where it was, frantically searches round.
Magus looks on without Yelena being aware of his presence.
Eventually, Yelena abandons her search and collapses into despair.
Pause. The Family begin to appear.

Family *(sotto voce)*   Yelena.

Family   Yelena.

Family   Yelena

Yelena   I've lost him now. I've lost him forever.

Family   Don't be afraid.

Family   Nothing is for ever.

Yelena   I lost the disc. It was the only thing I had to do and I lost it. I let it go.

Family   It's alright.

Family   We have come to help you.

Family *(all)*   We are your family.

Yelena   There's nothing you can do. There's nothing anyone can do. He doesn't even remember who I am.

Family   Then make him.

Family   Make him remember.

Yelena   I can't. I lost the disc – the pathway. I've no way of bringing him back.

Family   Then go to him.

Yelena   What?

Family   Isn't it obvious?

Family   If he cannot come to you.

Family   You must go to him.

Yelena   He's in the Otherworld. A world where time stands still. I can't follow him there!

Family   Why not?

Family   You've crossed borders before.

Family   Many of them.

Family   Don't be afraid.

Family	You will not be alone.
Family	We will go with you.
Family	Be strong.
Family	Go there.
Family	Cross the border.
Family	Find the one you love.
Family	Make him remember.

Music in. Magus raises the disc. Aims it at Yelena. Projection of rainbow lights.

Magus   Enter the land where time stands still.

Lights and music fade out.
End of Act One.

ACT TWO

Music in – magical, dream-like, as in the opening of the play.
Light up on Magus. Costume is the same as in Act 1 but now played by a different actor. He is holding the disc.

In the background, the projection of rainbow lights.

Magus   In a time beyond time
                     In a land beyond land

Magus aims the disc at an area of the stage.

Magus   Enter the circle of rainbow light.

He draws the Demons on stage (same costume/masks as Act 1).

With the disc aimed in the same direction ...

Magus	Enter the land where time stands still.

Callum is drawn on stage, accompanied by more Demons. He is dressed in present day clothes and played by a different actor. Magus aims the disc in a different direction.

Magus	Enter the realm of memory lost.

He draws Freya on stage, costume the same as in Act 1 but played by a different actress. She stares straight at Magus – the only one to show any awareness of his presence. Magus lowers the disc.

Magus	Enter the world of dreams.

Music and projection fade out. Magus exits.

Freya	Welcome, warrior of the clan.
Demons	Welcome to the Otherworld.

Lights come up on the Otherworld. Physical location is recognisably the same as Act 1 but with a few visible changes to denote a change to present day. However Callum's staff remains where he left it at the end of Act 1.

In the background we see projections of the present-day world. Trains. Planes. Motorways. Skyscrapers. Computers. 24-hour news. Mobile phones. Luxury holidays. Space travel. Etc. Etc. A world living beyond its means. Callum looks on incredulous.

Freya	I trust it meets with your approval.

Demon	A chieftain's crown upon your head.
Demon	A horse that rides the wind.
Demon	The sweetest music will fill your ears.
Callum	I never believed such things could exist. Is all this real?
Freya	Do your eyes not tell you so?
Callum	Your face ...
Freya	Is my appearance not pleasing to you?
Demon	Goddess of Beauty.
Demon	Goddess of Desire.
Callum	It seems different ... changed.
Demon	She is the face in your dreams.

Callum notices his present day clothes.

Callum	These clothes ... (*He studies his hands. Touches his face.*) Am I changed?
Freya	All things change. Don't you know that?
Callum	I don't feel different. (*He catches sight of the wooden staff. Picks it up. Half remembers it.*) This was mine ...
Freya	The world you came from has yet to happen.
Callum	I must return to my post.
Demon	There is no going back.
Demon	No leaving.
Demon	You gave your word.
Demon	Warrior of the clan.
Callum (*relents*)	How long have I been here?

Freya   From the beginning of course.

Callum   There was ...

Freya   What? What was there?

Callum   A girl.

Freya   What girl? What is her name?

Callum   ... I don't know. I can't remember.

Freya   Do you remember her face? Her appearance?
(*He tries but can't.*) Then there can be nothing to prevent our
betrothal.

Callum   Betrothal?

Demon   The fairest of beauties will dance as your bride.

Freya   Is that not why you came? Is that not the reason
you are here?

Demon   Goddess of Beauty.

Demon   Goddess of Desire.

Demon   The face in your dreams.

Freya (*offering him her hand*) Come. Join me in the dance of
matrimony.

Callum (*not taking it*) This is not what I agreed.

Freya   Is there some objection? Something that stands
in our way?

Callum   I came out of curiosity, that's all. I wanted to
find out if the old men's tales were true.

Freya   The old men's tales are as nothing.

Demon   A chieftain's crown upon your head.

Demon   A horse that rides the wind.

Freya   You will see things no member of your clan has
ever seen.

Again the staff serves as a memory prompt.

Callum	I cannot stay. I must return to my post. I must guard the border.

He turns to go. The Demons immediately move to stop him.

Demon	Would you break your word?
Demon	Warrior of the clan?
Freya	Until dawn. Tomorrow.

She waits for him to relent.

Callum	Until dawn ... And then I go.

Freya and Demons exit. Callum is left alone. Music in. Callum studies the staff. He tries to remember how to use it then begins to practice some of the moves we saw earlier.

Magus appears in the same position he was in at the end of Act 1. Callum has no awareness of him. Magus has the games disc. He directs it to a point on the set.

Magus	Enter the land where time stands still.

Yelena enters. Different actress. Present-day costume.

Magus	Enter the world of dreams.

Music fades out. Magus exits. Callum continues with his weapons practice.

Yelena *(struggling to recognise him)* Callum? Callum, is it you?

The staff prompts Callum into automatic 'on guard' mode.

Callum   Who is it? Who goes there?... Speak! Declare
yourself!

Yelena   Callum. It's me. Yelena. I've come to take you
back.

Callum   Who are you? ... If you're an exile ...

Yelena   We're both exiles, Callum. We're not from here.
This is not our world. Come. Come with me.

Callum   I know you, don't I? ... I've met you before.

Yelena   We were lovers. In a different world. Don't you
remember? We were lovers.

Callum   Lovers?

Yelena   You don't belong here, Callum. Neither of us do.

*She moves up to him. Gently takes the staff from his hands. Lays it
down. Takes his hand.*

Yelena   She wants you to forget. She wants to take away
your memory. (*She touches him in a way that repeats the closeness
and tenderness they had in the opening scene of the play.*)
You remember. I know you do.

Callum   What's your name?

Yelena   You know what it is.

Callum   ... Yel-ena ...

Yelena   She can't have you. I won't let her. Come. Come
with me. Now.

Lucca (*calling from off*) Callum!

Callum (*urgent*)   You have to go.

Yelena   No. I came to find you. I came to take you back.

Callum   Don't you understand? You're not safe here.

Logan *(calling from off)* Callum, are you there!

Yelena   Come with me, Callum. Come now.

Callum   I gave my word.

Yelena   Please, Callum. You must.

Drake *(calling from off)* Callum!

Callum   Tomorrow. I'll see you at dawn tomorrow.

Yelena   There is no tomorrow. Not here. You have to
believe me, Callum. Time stands still in the Otherworld. You must
come now!

Darla *(calling from off)* Callum!

Callum   Go, Yelena!... Go!

He pushes her off stage. Rolo enters.

Rolo   Here! I've found him! Over here! He's here!

*The rest of Callum's companions enter. Lucca, Logan, Drake Darla
and Magus. All dressed in present day fashion and played by different
actors. Magus is as we've already seen him.*

*Lucca, Logan, Drake, Darla, and Rolo hastily form a line. Magus
stays to one side. When they're ready...*

Lucca   We are the bearers of momentous news.

Logan   News of the utmost magnitude.

Drake   And tremendous portent.

Darla	Not to say of immense import.
Rolo	And very important.
Lucca	News of an earth-shattering nature.
Logan	Unprecedented.
Drake	Unbelievable and unforeseen.
Darla	Not to say of unparalleled unpredictability.
Rolo	And very unusual.
Lucca	News of paramount significance.
Logan	Of the most far-reaching consequence.
Drake	Of fundamental relevance.
Darla	Not to say of supreme pertinence.
Rolo	And very –

Callum *(interrupting)* Who are you? (*They are stopped in their tracks.*) Do I know you?

Pause. They glance at each other. Then the penny drops.

Lucca	Ah, I get it ... Nice one, Callum.
Logan	Had us fooled there for a mo.
Drake	Thought you'd come off the rails.
Darla	Not to say lost your marbles.
Rolo	You were joking.
Callum	What do you want?

Lucca *(takes a deep breath)* A new game has been invented.

Logan	Devised by my good self
Drake	No.
Darla	I devised it.
Drake	No you didn't.

Lucca the deviser.	There can be no dispute about the identity of
Darla	Excuse me.
Lucca	You're no trying to claim it was you I hope?
Darla	Who did the animation?
Drake	Nothing compared with the programming.
Logan	The sound track is what makes it.
Lucca	It's a dog's dinner.
Darla	What makes it is the graphics!
Drake	They wouldn't exist without my software skills.
Lucca	The only thing that makes it is the –

Callum *(interrupting)* Stop! *(They all stop.)* I haven't the first clue what any of you are talking about.

Rolo	I know. I'm no good at computers either.
Callum	… You've invented a game?
Lucca paranormal.	Set in a fantasy world of the supernatural and
Logan	A world of witch queens and demons.
Drake	Goddesses of Beauty and Desire.
Darla memory is lost.	Not to say, a land where time stands still and
Rolo	The Otherworld.
Lucca Darla.	We're all in it. Every one of us. Logan, Drake,
Logan	Lucca.
Lucca	Even Rolo.
Rolo	And you. You're in it too.
Callum	Me?

Drake	As some sort of border guard.
Darla	Not to say 'Warrior of the clan'
Rolo	Very swashbuckling.
Lucca	Even better – you have a lover.
Logan	A refugee.
Drake	A migrant.
Darla	Not to say, an exile.
Rolo	Very gorgeous.

Lucca   You meet in your dreams, then come together in a world of the future.

Logan   After the great climate change.

Drake   After the melting of the ice-caps and the raising of the ocean.

Darla   Not to say the wars of hunger and the collapse of civilisation.

Rolo	Her name is Yelena.
Callum	... Yelena?
Lucca	Magus came up with that.
Callum	Magus ...
Logan	He created the character profiles.
Drake	Structured the plot.
Darla	Not to say shaped the narrative.
Rolo	He wrote the story.

Callum (*looking at Magus*) The Storyteller ... This game?... What's it called? What's it about?

They all look to Rolo. He produces a games disc. Holds it up for Callum to see.

Callum   ... Rainbow lights ...

Lucca   Precisely. That's what all of us think it should be called.

Logan   But not Magus.

Drake   He thinks it should be named after some ancient Celtic goddess.

Darla   Not to say, mythological shape changer.

Rolo   The Cailleach.

Callum   And this is it? This disc? This is a game?

Lucca   The one and only. The master copy.

Callum   Why have you brought it to me?

Lucca   You played no part in its production.

Logan   You have no vested interest

Drake   Who else better to act as defender and protector?

Darla   Not to say safe keeper and sentinel.

Rolo   We'd like you to guard it for us.

Lucca   Can't risk the competition getting their hands on it. *(Takes the disk from Rolo and hands it to Callum.)* The future of interactive entertainment lies in your hands.

All exit except Callum and Magus.

Callum   Magus.

Magus   I'm pleased you remember.

Callum   The Storyteller. This world I've come to ... The Otherworld.

Magus   What about it?

Callum   Is it a dream? Imagination? Have I travelled back in time? Or is it something to do with this – this game you've created?

Magus   Maybe it's all of them. Dreams. Games.
Imagination. Time. It's not impossible to be in several worlds at
once.

Callum   How can you be in more than one world?

Magus   You always want things to be simple. Clearly
defined borders. It isn't always as easy as that, Callum. Even you can
find yourself in a strange world. An exile... Or in love with one.

Callum   Yelena?

Magus   Isn't falling in love entering a different world?
Enjoy it. Allow yourself to dream. Cross the border.

Callum   She came here for me. She wanted me to go
with her. She says time stands still in the Otherworld. Is that true?
Is that possible?

Magus   Wait for tomorrow and you may end up waiting
forever ... Isn't that what they say?

Callum   All these incredible things I've seen ... Winged
horses flying through the sky. Palaces of silver. All this abundance.
I never believed such things were possible.

Demons start to appear.

Demon   A world beyond imagining.

Demon   A world of luxury.

Demon   A world of wealth.

Demon   A world of dreams.

Callum *(to Magus)* And them? The demons. Are they from this land
where time stands still?

Demon   A chieftain's crown upon your head.

Demon   A horse that rides the wind.

Callum   Or are they part of this game of yours?

Magus   I think it might be better if I take care of that, don't you? *(He takes the disc.)* I think you know where the demons are from, Callum. Some borders even you cannot guard.

Magus exits.

Demon	Come.
Demon	Follow me.
Demon	Follow me over.
Callum	What do you want with me? Why did you bring me here?
Demon	You came of your own free will.
Demon	To find out.
Demon	To judge for yourself.
Demon	To see what no member of your clan has ever seen.
Demon	And return to tell the tale.
Demon	Your name famed throughout the land.
Demon	Your deeds spoken of for generations to come.
Demon	Tomorrow at dawn you will be back at your post.
Demon	Guarding the border.
Demon	Come.
Demon	Follow me.
Demon	Follow me over.
Demon	Have you no spirit of adventure?
Demon	No sense of daring?
Demon	You're not afraid, are you?
Demon	Warrior of the clan?

Callum hesitates a moment longer then goes with them. They all exit. Yelena enters with caution.

Yelena   Callum?... Callum, are you there? *(She notices the staff which Callum has left behind.)* Callum ...!

She searches round. The Family begin to appear.

Family   He is not here.

Family   You will not find him.

Family   He has gone.

Yelena   Gone?

Family   Don't be afraid.

Family   We are here to help you.

Yelena   Gone where? Where is he? What's happened to him?

Family   He is alright.

Family   He is unharmed.

Yelena   Is he with her?

Yelena   He is, isn't he? He's with her. With Freya. Why does he go to her? Why does he stay in this world?

Family   He gave his word.

Family   He does not want to be thought of as lacking courage.

Family   Of being afraid.

Family   Of running away.

Yelena   And her?... Freya? What about her? What is she to him?

Family   Even the most faithful of lovers can find themselves flattered by the attentions of another.

Yelena   Is that what it is?... Have I lost him? Has she taken him from me?

Family   Only if you let her.

Family   Only if you give in.

Yelena   How can I stop her? This is not my world.

Family   You must be strong.

Family   Fight for him.

Family   You love him, don't you?

Family   Then fight for him.

Family start to exit.

Yelena   Where are you going?... Don't leave me. You can't go. I need your help!

Family   Don't be afraid.

Family   Be strong.

Family   Fight for him.

Family exit. Zita and Carmen enter. Played by different actors in present-day costume. Yelena doesn't immediately know who they are.

Zita   Here you are. Where have you been? We've looked all over.

Carmen   Yelena. Are you OK? Is everything alright?

Zita   Is no one with you?

Yelena   No.

Carmen *(glancing round)* Are you sure?

Zita   We heard your voice.

Carmen   Did you call us?

Yelena   No.

Carmen   You didn't?

Zita   We thought you were in trouble.

Carmen   We've been going off our heads.

Yelena   Zita?

Zita   What?

Yelena   Is it you?... And Carmen?

Zita and Carmen share an anxious glance.

Zita   Yelena, are you alright? Has something
happened? Tell us. What's wrong? What is it?

Yelena   Nothing. Nothing – I'm fine. I'm alright.

Carmen   You don't look it.

Zita   What are you doing here anyway?

Yelena   I've come to find Callum.

Zita   Callum?

Yelena   You haven't seen him, have you?

Carmen   Who's Callum?

Yelena   You know who he is. *(Blank looks from Zita and
Carmen.)* The one I told you about. A warrior of the clan. I have to
find him.

Carmen *(bemused)*   A warrior of the clan?

Yelena   I know what you think. I don't care. I love him
that's all that matters. I don't care what you say.

Zita   Yelena. What are you talking about?

Carmen   This Callum ... How long have you known him?

Yelena   Why do you keep asking me these things? Don't
you understand, he's with her – he's with Freya.

Carmen   Who?

Yelena   She brought him here. He doesn't realise that
time stands still in the Otherworld. I have to find him. I have to
make him remember.

Zita and Carmen are now seriously worried.

Zita   Yelena, you've got to stop talking like this.
People will begin to think you're ... *(stops herself)*

Yelena   What? What will they begin to think? That I'm
mad? That's what the two of you think, isn't it. You think I'm losing
my wits.

Carmen   No – No, Yelena, we don't. We don't at all.

Zita   All these people you invent. Stories you make
up. Lovers. Warriors. Lands where time stands still. Sometimes I
think you live in a different world. *(Pause.)*

Yelena   What happened to our family?

Zita   Yelena ...

Yelena   What happened to them? I want to know.

Zita   You know what happened to them. *(Pause.)*
They were killed. All of them. They were taken from our home and
... *(She stops, unable to continue).*

Carmen   It was a long time ago, Yelena. In a different
country. It happened to many of us. We were the lucky ones. We
managed to get out. We came here. This is our home now.

Yelena   They visit me.

Zita   What?

Yelena   Our family. All of them. They talk to me. They look after me. They say they'll keep me safe. They come to help me.

Pause.

Carmen   Yelena ... Listen to me ... You're not the only one to think thoughts like that ... It happens to all of us ... Terrible things occurred. Things none of us can ever get over. Not if we live to be a hundred. You're not going mad. You're not losing your wits. You have to believe that. And you do have a family. Not just the one in your head. A real family ... Zita. And me ... We're your family. We'll always be your family.

Zita   Come with us. Back to the flat.

Yelena   Flat?

Carmen   Where we live.

Yelena   We live in a shelter in the woods.

Zita   Please, Yelena. No more inventions.

Carmen   Just come with us.

Yelena   No ... No, I can't. I have to find Callum. That's why I've come here. I won't let her take him from me.

She hurries off. Zita and Carmen watch her go. Carmen gives Zita a comforting hug. They exit. Music. Lighting change. Freya appears. Demons enter with Callum.

Demon   Goddess of Beauty.

Demon   Goddess of Desire.

Demon   The face in your dreams.

Callum   Who are you?... Something I've imagined?

A vision in my mind? Or are you part of this game?

Freya	Game?
Callum	The one they asked me to guard. The one Magus created.
Freya	You have been speaking to the Storyteller?
Callum	Is that it? Is that what you are? A character in this game of his?
Freya	Magus is a charlatan. You must believe nothing he says.
Callum	There's a girl. An exile. Her name is Yelena.
Freya	She does not exist. The girl is a fantasy.
Callum	She and I are lovers.
Freya	Your mind is playing tricks on you. She does not exist.
Callum	No. She's real. I know she is. I shall go back with her. Now.
Freya	These are false memories. Look into my eyes.

Music in. Haunting. Hypnotic.

Demons	Look.
Freya	Are you afraid?
Demon	Have you no courage?
Demon	Are you a coward?
Demon	Warrior of the clan?

Unable to resist their challenge, Callum looks into her eyes.

Freya   Tell me what you see. *(Almost immediately he
     begins to fall under her spell.)*

Callum   Rainbow lights ...

Demon   She is the circle of rainbow light.

Freya   And what do you hear?

Callum   Music.

Demon   She is the mist that clouds your thought.

Demon   She is the worm in your mind.

Demon   She is the vision that blurs your sight.

Demon   She is the end of time.

Demon   She is the dark of memory lost.

*Callum is overcome by the spell. The Demons lift him bodily. Gently
lay him down.*

Freya   Sleep well, warrior of the clan. When you awake
     your mind will be clear. And you will join me in the dance of
     matrimony.

*Music fades out as Freya and Demons exit. Callum remains sleeping.
Yelena enters.*

Yelena   Callum! *(She runs to him, tries to wake him.)*
     Callum. Callum, wake up! It's alright, Callum. I'm here, I've found
     you. It's alright. Everything's going to be alright.

The Family start to appear.

Family   You cannot wake him.

Yelena	Callum ... Callum, wake up!
Family	You cannot wake him.
Yelena	I have to. I have to tell him I'm here. Callum!
Family	You cannot wake him.
Yelena	I won't give up. I won't let her take him from me!
Family *(all)*	You cannot wake him.

Yelena   Callum ... Callum! *(She struggles on until finally she realises it's hopeless and gives up.)* What's wrong? ... Why won't he wake? *(sudden panic)* He's not...?

Family	No.
Family	Sleeping.
Family	Only sleeping.
Yelena	I have to speak to him. I have to make him remember.
Family	Then do it.
Family	Speak to him.
Family	Make him remember.
Yelena	He's asleep.
Family	Have you forgotten where you met?
Yelena	What do you mean?
Family	In your dreams.
Family	You met in your dreams.
Yelena	How does that help?
Family	Meet him again.
Family	As you did before.
Yelena	In his dreams?
Family	Speak to him.

Family   Make him remember.

Pause. Music in.

Yelena   Callum ... Callum, listen to me.

No reaction from Callum. Yelena hesitates, looks to the Family.

Family   Go on.

Family   Be strong.

Family   Speak to him.

Yelena   Remember, Callum. Remember the one you
love. The one who loves you. Remember who she is. Remember her
face.

Family   The face in your dreams

Yelena   The one you love – Callum

Family   The face in your dreams.

Yelena   The one who loves you.

Family   The face in your dreams.

Yelena   Remember the face in your dreams.

She kisses her fingers and touches his cheek. Music fades out.

Yelena   Do you think he heard?

Family   He heard.

Yelena   What now? What do I do next?

Family   You must not stay here.

Yelena	I can't leave him.
Family	It will not be safe.
Family	Come back.
Family	Come back to him later.

Family start to move away.

Yelena	Where are you going?... You're not leaving?
Family	You have done what you came to do.
Family	We are no longer necessary.
Yelena	What do you mean?
Family	You are strong now.
Family	You no longer need us.
Yelena	You're coming back though? You're not leaving for good?
Family	You have your own family.
Family	Your real family.
Family	Zita.
Family	And Carmen.
Yelena	But you're my family too. I need you. I need your help.
Family	You did.
Family	But not now.
Family	Not any more.
Yelena	Not goodbye. I don't want it to be goodbye. Please ...
Family	You are strong.

Family	You no longer need us.
Yelena	I don't want this. I don't want you to go.
Family	You will never be alone.
Family	Always think of us.
Family	Always remember us.
Family *(all)*	We are your family.

Family exit. Yelena watches them go. Pause. She turns back to Callum then exits. Freya enters with the Demons. Approaches Callum.

Freya	You may awaken, warrior of the clan.
Demon	Enter the realm of memory lost.

Callum stirs and wakes up.

Callum	Is it dawn?
Freya	There is no dawn here.
Callum	... I had such dreams.
Freya	And what did your dreams tell you?

Callum *(struggling to recall)* They told me to remember the one I love.

Freya	And do you? Who is she? Who is the one you love?
Callum	... Remember the face in your dreams.
Freya	The face in your dreams?

Demons *(sotto voce)* She is the face in your dreams.

Freya	You are certain of this? She is the one?

Callum	She is the one.
Demons *(building)*	She is the face in your dreams.
Freya	Swear to me this is true. It is her, you love? Her and no other.
Demons	She is the face in your dreams.
Callum	On my word as a warrior.
Demons	She is the face in your dreams.
Freya	Then your dreams will come true, warrior of the clan.

Music in. Projection of rainbow lights. During the following, the demons whirl Callum around in chaotic fashion. At the same time, Freya disappears to be replaced by the Cailleach.

Demons *(chant)*	She is the circle of rainbow light.
	She is the face in your dreams.
	She is the mist that clouds your thought.
	She is the worm in your mind.
	She is the vision that blurs your sight.
	She is the end of time.
	She is the dark of memory lost.
	She is The Cailleach.
	Cailleach Bheur.

The Cailleach appears. Music and projection fade out. She offers Callum her hand.

The Cailleach	Come. Join me in the dance of matrimony.
Callum	Who are you?
Demon	Goddess of Beauty.
Demon	Goddess of Desire.

Demon   The face in your dreams.

Callum   You?

Demon   She is the Cailleach.

Demons   Cailleach Bheur.

Callum   It was you? All along? From the beginning? You
were Freya?

The Cailleach   Your eyes saw only what they wished to
see. And they may see the same again. Freya can be yours whenever
you choose.

Callum   You think that's why I came here? For Freya?
You've no hold on me. I'll leave this world. I'll return to my post.

The Demons immediately stop him.

Demon   You gave your word.

Demon   Warrior of the clan

Demon   She is the one you love.

Demon   She is the face in your dreams.

Yelena enters.

Yelena   No, she isn't!... Don't listen to them, Callum.
They split us apart once before. Don't let it happen again.

The Cailleach   You!

Yelena   Remember the one you love, Callum. Remember
the one who loves you.

Callum   Yelena. (*They move towards each other. The
Demons immediately step between them.*) Let me through! Let me
pass!

The Cailleach   You made a vow, warrior of the clan. You gave your word!

Callum   My vow was to Yelena. She is the face in my dreams. She is the one I love.

The Cailleach   Then your love is worthless. The girl has no place in this world.

Music in. Powerful and magical. Projection of rainbow lights.

Callum   What are you doing?

The Cailleach points a finger at Yelena and begins to invoke a spell. At the same time the Demons seize Yelena and lift her into the air while others prevent Callum reaching her.

The Cailleach   Come yarrow come rue
Bladderwrack and feverfew
Come scullcap come squill
Witchhazel and dill
Come hyssop come hops
Snake root and moss
Come spell of demon
And devil's eye
And take this soul to another time!

Demons   She is the dark of memory lost!
She is the Cailleach!
Cailleach Bheur!

Music and projection build to a climax as the Demons carry Yelena off.

Callum   Yelena!.....

Music and projection fade out.

Callum   You think this will make me stay? I'll find her. I
    don't care where they've taken her. I'll find her!

The Cailleach   You will find nothing.
                  You will remember nothing.
                  Look into my eyes.

Music in. Haunting. Hypnotic.

Demon   She is the circle of rainbow light

Demons   She is the face in your dreams.

Callum tries to escape but the demons keep a tight hold on him.

The Cailleach   Are you afraid? Warrior of the clan?

Demon   She is the mist that clouds your thought

Demons   She is the worm in your mind

The Cailleach   Look into my eyes. (*The demons try to*
    force him to look.)

Demon   She is the vision that blurs your sight.

Demons   She is the end of time.

The Cailleach   Look.

Demon   She is the dark of memory lost.

Magus suddenly appears.

Magus　　　　Guard the border, Callum!

Music ends abruptly.

Demons　　　　The Storyteller ...

Magus　　　　The realm of memory lost is a world you'd do well to avoid.

The Cailleach　　　　There is nothing you can do, Magus. He belongs to me. He will stay here for ever.

Magus　　　　Perhaps you've forgotten who controls the pathway.

The Cailleach　　　　You have no power over me. I have my own pathway and I can send you along it as easily as I sent the girl.

Magus　　　　Spells and magic is it?

The Cailleach　　　　Time to show which of us is the stronger.

Music in. She aims a finger at Magus.

The Cailleach　　　　Come yarrow come rue

Demons　　　　Bladderwrack and feverfew

The Cailleach　　　　Come scullcap come squill

Demons　　　　Witchhazel and dill

The Cailleach　　　　Come hyssop come hops

Demons　　　　Snake root and moss

The Cailleach　　　　Come spell of demon

Demons　　　　And devil's eye

The Cailleach　　　　And take this soul ...

Magus　　　　Isn't there something you've overlooked?

*Magus produces the disc and aims it at the Cailleach.
At the same time, Callum's companions appear.*

Lucca   Characters can be changed.

Logan   Storylines altered.

Drake   Profiles re-written.

Darla   Not to say discarded completely.

Rolo   Are you sure you want to permanently delete
        this character?

*The Demons release Callum and shrink away, leaving the Cailleach
alone and isolated.*

Magus   Nothing is for ever. Not even a character in a
        game.

*Pause. The Cailleach weighs up her options before realising she's
beaten.*

The Cailleach   Take him. Do with him as you wish.
        (to Callum) Time will be your jailor, warrior of the clan.

Projection fades out. The Cailleach and Demons exit.

Callum's companions celebrate.

Lucca   Y – e – s!

Logan   Result!

Drake   Get in there!

Darla   Not to say – you beauty!

Rolo   Champions!

Callum   A game? Is that what all this has been?...
Demons? The Cailleach? The Otherworld?... Just a game? Re-
inventing yourselves in a world where time stands still and everyone
has two lives? Well, congratulations, all of you. You had me fooled.
Hook, line and sinker. So what now, Storyteller? Where next? Back
to reality is it? Open a pathway and we all wake up?

Magus   It isn't finished yet.

Callum   What?

Magus   There's another level ... The game isn't over.

Callum   Well, what do you know? More fool me. Why
didn't I guess?

Magus   We inhabit many worlds, Callum... Times.
Places. Dreams. Games. States of mind. Sometimes we go there by
choice. Sometimes because there's no alternative. The border
between fantasy and reality is one even you have difficulty guarding.

Callum   Always the clever answer. Alright then, Magus.
Go ahead. Take us to the next level. But just one thing ... When your
game is over. When that disc of yours is no longer needed ... do
something for me, will you?

Magus   If I'm able.

Callum   Bury it. Dig a hole in the ground. And bury it.

Magus   Are you certain that's what you want?

Callum   Bury it deep.

Magus   Then it will be done.

*Magus holds up the disc. Music in – mysterious and magical, as at the
start of the play. Projection of rainbow lights.*

The five companions exit. Callum remains on stage.

Magus   In a time beyond time
                             In a land beyond land.

Both Yelenas (Act 1 & 2) appear and Callum (Act 1).

All five actors stand separate from one another at various points around the set. Magus aims the disc at an area of the stage.

Magus   Enter the circle of rainbow light.

A third Yelena is drawn in. Different actor, different costume, different time. She repeats Yelena's movements at the start of the play. Looks around as if hoping to meet someone. Magus aims the disc in a different direction.

Magus   Enter the world of dreams.

A third Callum is drawn in. Different actor, different costume, different time. Callum and Yelena repeat the same movements as at the start of the play. They are overjoyed to see each other. They move towards one another, hold hands. They embrace, celebrate their re-union.

Magus aims the disc in another direction.

Magus   Enter the land where time stands still.

The Demons are drawn in. They watch Callum and Yelena closely. Magus aims the disc in yet another direction.

Magus   Enter the realm of memory lost.

The Cailleach is drawn in. Magus and the Cailleach stare straight at each other. They hold the image – a repeat of the opening – the two lovers and the opposing forces of the Cailleach and Magus.

Lights down.
The end.

SMALL FRY

Premiered by pupils of Park Grove Primary School, York

Martha Colcutt

Ned Martin

Niamh Brannigan

Daniel Young

Imogen Stone

Monica Thirlway

Oliver Dowker

Lizzy Hall

Hazel Rawcliffe

Robert Mason

Ruth Harvey

Eleanor Katsarelis

Christian Brennan

Hetty Webster

Miranda King

Otto Davey

India Rose

Katy Ross

William Bunch-Merrick

Owen Green

Hannah Glowala

Martha Wood Saanaoui

Kiera Power

Aaron Saint John

Oliver Avery

Jack Berry

Jack Talbot

David Bialochleb

SMALL FRY

Small Fry

When Juliet Forster from York Theatre Royal first rang to ask if I'd be interested in writing a short youth theatre play as part of **The Playhouse Project** *(see below)*, I'd just finished reading *Barbarians at the Gate* by Bryan Burrough and John Helyer. It's a jaw-dropping account of what was then the largest corporate take-over in American history.

In 1988, over a period of two months, a battle of astonishing proportions took place for control of RJR Nabisco. The rules were simple – never pay in cash, never tell the truth, and never play by the rules. What took place became a symbol of the greed and power-mongering of the 1980s. Predators and Scavengers scrapped it out in a no-holds-barred fight to the finish.

What struck me most about the story was the gulf in values – call it morality if you will – between how most of us try to live our lives and what passes for normal in the world of high finance.

Juliet gave me a free hand in terms of subject matter, but there was only one thing I wanted to write about. The play is a fantasy, the characters are animal-like, the plot is simple, but the values are the same.

The Playhouse Project involved:

College Road Primary School, Plymouth (director Jo Harvey)

Dundee Rep Youth Theatre, Dundee (director Gemma Nicol)

Park Grove Primary School, York (director Jill Campbell)

Stanley Park Junior School, Carshalton (director Larry Brown)

SMALL FRY

Commissioned by York Theatre Royal for The Playhouse Project. First performed at York Theatre Royal, Dundee Rep, Plymouth Theatre Royal and Polka Theatre for Children, Wimbledon, May to July 2008. Directed by Jill Campbell, Gemma Nicol and Larry Brown.

CHARACTERS

Characters are neither human nor animal, but a mixture of both. The cast size and the number of people performing in any group are entirely flexible depending on requirements. Lines and speeches can be split up and allocated as required.

The Dragon – a single character played by a group of actors moving and performing as one.
Predators – a group of squabbling individuals, like a pack of wolves.
Scavengers – another squabbling group. a flock of gulls, a troop of monkeys. Numbers flexible.
Small Fry – a group of three individuals.
Chorus – the whole company at the beginning of the play. Characters emerge from the chorus at the appropriate time.
Percussionists – completely flexible. Could double as actors if required.

SET: Can be very simple. No specific requirements beyond a few props.

COSTUMES: Can be as simple or elaborate as desired. There should be some sort of visual identification for Predators and Scavengers. Also for the Dragon and Small Fry. But this could be as simple as a colour, badge or logo.

MOVEMENT: Each group or character should have its own identifiable movement which should be heightened and stylised.

PERCUSSION: Used wherever appropriate to heighten mood and drama and to provide a rhythm for movement. If at all possible it should be played live by the children.

ACT ONE
Percussion in. Chorus appears.

Chorus   Imagine a place.
                               A place that is as much here as it is there.
                               Imagine a time.
                               A time that is as much now as it was then.
                               In this place and time this time and place
                               Rules Are Simple.
                               Rules Are Few.
                               Rule One.
                               Take What You Want.
                               Snatch It.
                               Grab It.
                               It's Yours.
                               It Belongs To You.
                               Rule Two.
                               Never
                               never ever
                               never never ever
                               tell the truth.
                               Rule three.
                               Trust no one.
                               Not your friend.
                               Not your brother.
                               Not your sister.
                               Not your mother.
                               Not each other.
                               In this time and place
                               this place and time
                               only one thing counts.
                               The only things that counts –
                               is money.
                               Money.
                               Money.
                               Money!
                               In this place and time
                               this time and place

men are animals
and animals men.
Here be ...

Predators *(all)*   Predators!

Predators leap out from the Chorus. Swaggering, boastful, bullying, aggressive. Movement and percussion to match.

Predator   Sharp-eyed

Predator   sharp-clawed

Predator   menacing

Predators *(all)*   Predators!

Predator   Stealthy

Predator   stalking

Predator   deadly

Predators *(all)*   Predators!

Predator   On the prowl

Predators *(all)*   Predators!

Predator   Ready to pounce

Predators *(all)*   Predators!

Predator   In for the kill

Predators *(all)*   Predators!! *(Predators swagger off.)*

Chorus   In this place and time this time and place
Men are animals and animals men.
Here be ...

Scavengers *(all)*   Scavengers!

Scavengers appear from the Chorus. Thieving, deceitful, fast moving, full of tricks. Movement and percussion to match.

Scavenger	Cunning
Scavenger	Quick
Scavenger	Never miss a trick
Scavengers *(all)*	Scavengers!
Scavenger	Crafty
Scavenger	Devious
Scavenger	Wheeler-dealing
Scavengers *(all)*	Scavengers!
Scavenger	Nifty
Scavengers *(all)*	Scavengers!
Scavenger	Light-fingered
Scavengers *(all)*	Scavengers!
Scavenger	Thieving
Scavengers *(all)*	Scavengers! *(Scavengers tumble off).*
Chorus	Finally in this place and time always close in this time and place lurking in the shadows...

The Dragon begins to emerge from the Chorus. Played by a group of actors moving together. Dark, threatening, malevolent. Movement and percussion to match.

Dragon	I am the want that can never be met.
	I am the hunger for more.
	I am the glut that is never enough
	I am the plenty of plenty
	I am the fever that poisons your mind
	I am the love of possession
	Neither human nor animal am I.
	Neither living nor dead.
	This place and time
	this time and place
	belong to me.
	I am the Dragon.
	Dragon!
	They think they're free to pick and choose
	but this is a game of heads I win
	and tails they lose.
	I'll have them for breakfast
	I'll swallow them whole
	I'll chew on their flesh
	And spit out their bones.

(*The Dragon produces a large pot with 'JACKPOT' written on the side. The Dragon places it in a prominent position on the set.*)

	They'll cheat and lie and fight and steal
	to get their hands on this tempting prize.
	But in the scrum and scramble
	they won't realize
	that it's a trap.
	And the moment they count one two three
	every last one will become part of me.
	I am the Dragon.
	Dragon!

The Dragon exits. Scavengers return.

Scavengers *(all)*	Scavengers!
Scavenger	Cunning.

Scavenger	Quick.
Scavenger	Never miss a trick.
Scavengers *(all)*	Scavengers!

They discover the Jackpot.

Scavenger	What have we here?
Scavenger	Some kind of pot.
Scavenger	Big pot.
Scavenger	Pot with a lid.
Scavenger	Pot with writing on.
Scavenger *(struggles to read)* Jack...	
Scavenger	...pot
Scavenger	Jack Pot?
Scavenger	Jackpot.
Scavenger:	What's it mean?
Scavenger:	Money.
Scavenger:	It means money.
Scavengers *(all)*	Money?
Scavenger	Money in the pot.
Scavenger	Lots of money.
Scavenger	Pots of money.
Scavenger	Fountains of money.
Scavenger	Mountains of money.
Scavengers *(all)*	Money!
Scavenger	Steal it!
Scavenger	Take it!

Scavenger	Snatch it!
Scavenger	Grab it!
Scavenger	It belongs to me!
Scavenger	No it doesn't!
Scavenger	It belongs to me!
Scavenger	It's mine!
Scavenger	It's mine!
Scavenger	Mine!
Scavenger	Mine!
Scavenger	Mine!
Scavengers *(all)* lid.)	Mine!! *(Still squabbling they try to take off the lid.)*
Scavenger:	Stuck.
Scavenger	Twist and prise with main and might –
Scavenger	it won't come off
Scavenger	The lid's stuck tight. *(Others grab the pot.)*
Scavenger	Give it here!

As they're struggling to open the pot Predators arrive.

Predators *(all)*	Predators!

Scavengers immediately attempt to hide the pot. But Predators have already seen it.

Predator	Sharp-eyed
Predator	sharp-clawed

Predator	menacing
Predators *(all)*	Predators!
Predator	Hiding something?
Scavenger	Hiding?
Predator	Hiding!
Scavenger	Us?
Scavenger	What could we be hiding?

Predators push Scavengers roughly aside.

Predator	Nobody messes with us!
Predators *(all)*	Predators!

The pot is revealed.

Predator	What have we here?
Scavenger	Nothing.
Scavenger	It's nothing.
Predator	Some kind of pot.
Predator	Big pot.
Predator	Pot with a lid.
Predator	Pot with writing on.
Predator *(struggles to read)* Jack...
Predator	...pot
Predator	Jack Pot?
Predator	Jackpot.
Predator	What's it mean?

Scavenger	Nothing.
Scavenger	It means nothing.
Predator	Money.
Predator	It means money
Predators *(all)*	Money?
Predator	Money in the pot.
Predator	Lots of money.
Predator	Pots of money.
Predator	Fountains of money.
Predator	Mountains of money.
Predators *(all)*	Money!
Predator	Steal it!
Predator	Take it!
Predator	Snatch it!
Predator:	Grab it!
Predator	It belongs to me!
Predator	No it doesn't.
Predator	It belongs to me!
Predator	It's mine!
Predator	It's mine!
Predator	Mine!
Predator	Mine!
Predator	Mine!
Predators *(all)*	Mine!!

Still squabbling, the Predators try to pull off the lid.

Predator	Stuck.
Predator	Twist and prise with main and might –
Predator	it won't come off.
Predator	The lid's stuck tight.

Other Predators grab the pot.

Predator	Give it here!

Others try to pull of the lid.

Scavenger	There's nothing in.
Scavenger	Nothing at all.
Scavenger	Not even a flea.
Predator	Expect us to believe that?
Predator	This Jackpot is coming with me!
Predator	No it's not!
Predator	It's coming with me!
Predator	With me!
Predator	With me!
Predator	Me!
Predator	Me!
Predator	Me!
Predators *(all)*	Me!

Still squabbling, Predators chase off with the pot.

Scavenger	No money.
Scavenger	No pot.
Scavenger	What now?
Scavenger	Have to get it back.
Scavenger	Oh very clever.
Scavenger	From Predators?
Scavenger	How?

Small Fry enter. Open, friendly, cheerful, honest. Percussion and movement to match.

Small Fry *(all)*	Hello.
Scavenger	Who are you?
Small Fry *(all)*	Small Fry.
Scavenger	Small Fry?
Small Fry *(all)*	Small Fry.
Small Fry 1	Pleased to meet you.
Small Fry 2	How do you do.
Scavenger	Where're you from?
Scavenger	Not from here.
Scavenger	Not this place and time
Scavenger	this time and place.
Small Fry 3	Somewhere else.
Small Fry 1	Different place and time
Small Fry 2	time and place.
Scavenger	Can't come here, Small Fry.
Scavenger	Don't belong.

Scavenger	Small Fry not welcome.
Scavenger	So clear off.
Scavenger	Back where you came from.
Scavengers *(all)*	Vanish!
Small Fry 3	Sorry.
Small Fry 1	Very sorry.
Small Fry 2	Didn't mean to cause offence.

Small Fry start to go. But then Scavengers get an idea, exchange knowing glances.

Scavenger	Wait a minute ...
Scavenger	There might ...
Scavenger	possibly ...
Scavenger	be a way
Scavenger	for you to stay.
Scavenger	Stay for good.
Scavenger	With us.
Scavenger	All be friends.
Small Fry *(all, hopeful)* Friends?	
Scavenger	That depends.
Small Fry 3	Depends?
Scavenger	You see ...
Scavenger	... we have a slight problem.
Scavenger	We could use some help.
Small Fry 3	We'll help you.
Small Fry 1	We're good at helping.

Small Fry 2	What do you want us to do?
Scavenger	Someone's taken our pot.
Scavenger	Jackpot.
Small Fry 3	Jackpot?
Scavenger	Stolen it.
Scavenger	Borrowed it
Scavenger	to be exact.
Scavenger	But now we'd like it back.
Small Fry 1	Who's borrowed it?
Scavenger	Predators.
Small Fry *(all, alarmed)* Predators?	
Scavenger	Oh, don't worry!
Scavenger	Not sharp-eyed
Scavenger	sharp clawed
Scavenger	menacing Predators.
Scavenger	Soft
Scavenger	friendly
Scavenger	toothless Predators.
Scavenger	Bring back the Jackpot
Scavenger	and you can stay,
Scavenger	stay for good
Scavenger	with us.
Scavenger	All be friends.
Small Fry 2	Honest?
Scavenger	Would *we* lie?
Scavenger	It's a promise.
Scavenger	Scavengers' honour.

Small Fry 3	OK.
Small Fry 2	We'll do it.
Small Fry 1	We'll bring back the Jackpot.

Small Fry exit. Scavengers fall about laughing.

Scavenger	What a scam!
Scavenger	What a dinker!
Scavenger	The perfect con!
Scavenger *(all)*	Hook, line and sinker!

Scavengers exit laughing. Predators enter. Still trying to get the lid off the pot.

Predator	Stuck.
Predator	Twist and prise with main and might –
Predator	it won't come off.
Predator	The lid's stuck tight.

Small Fry enter.

Small Fry *(all)*	Hello.
Predator	Who are you?
Small Fry *(all)*	Small Fry.
Predator	Small Fry?
Small Fry *(all)*	Small Fry.
Small Fry 1	Pleased to meet you.

Small Fry 2	How do you do.
Predator	What're you doing here?
Small Fry 3	Come for the pot.
Predator	What?
Small Fry 1	Jackpot.
Small Fry 2	Please,
Small Fry 3	if that's alright.

Small Fry pick up the pot. Predators immediately snatch it back, become threatening.

Predator	What're you doing?!
Predator	Who d'you think you are?!
Predator	Nobody messes with us!
Predators *(all)*	Predators!
Predator	Sharp-eyed
Predator	sharp-clawed
Predator	menacing
Predators *(all)*	Predators!

Small Fry only laugh.

Small Fry *(all)*	No you're not.
Predator	What?
Small Fry 1	Not sharp-eyed
Small Fry 2	Sharp-clawed
Small Fry 3	Menacing Predators

Small Fry 1   Soft

Small Fry 2   Friendly

Small Fry 3   toothless Predators.

Predator   Soft?

Predator   Friendly?

Predator   ... Toothless?

Small Fry 1   Scavengers told us.

Predators *(all)*   Scavengers?

Small Fry 3 *(taking the pot)* They'd like their Jackpot back now please.

Predator *(snatching it back)* Oh they would, would they?!

Predator   Their Jackpot?!

Predators *(all)*   Scavengers!

Predator   You tell them this.

Predator   Scavengers!

Predator   This Jackpot belongs to me.

Predator   No it doesn't.

Predator   It belongs to me.

Predator   It's mine.

Predator   It's mine.

Predator   Mine!

Predator   Mine!

Predator   Mine!

Predators *(all)*   Mine!!!

Suddenly remembering Small Fry, they act aggressive.

Predator	What're you looking at?
Predator	Nobody messes with us.
Predators *(all)*	Predators!
Predator	Clear off!
Predator	Back where you came from!
Predators *(all)*	Vanish!

They chase Small Fry off and continue trying to get the lid off. But Small Fry return and watch from a hiding place.

Predator	Stuck.
Predator	Twist and prise with main and might
Predator	– it won't come off.
Predator	The lid's stuck tight.

Percussion announces the arrival of the Dragon.

Dragon	No point huffing and puffing pulling and pushing. Twist and prise with main and might the lid of the pot will stay on tight.
Predator	Who are you?
Dragon	Brute force will never succeed. To win the Jackpot A magic number is what you need.
Predator	Magic number?
Predator	What number?
Dragon	How much money?

Predators *(all)*	Money?
Dragon	In the pot. In the Jackpot. How much?
Predator *(hopeful)*	A hundred?
Dragon	More.
Predator	A thousand?
Dragon	Even more.
Predator	A million?!
Dragon	How many millions?
Predator	One?
Predator	Two?
Predators *(all)*	Three!

Instant percussion. During the following, the Dragon dances and whirls around the Predators weaving a spell which leaves them helpless to resist. One by one they lose their identity and are absorbed into the Dragon.

Dragon	They think they're free to pick and choose but this is a game of heads I win and tails they lose. I'll have them for breakfast I'll swallow them whole I'll chew on their flesh And spit out their bones. Neither human nor animal am I. Neither living nor dead. This place and time this time and place

belong to me.
I am The Dragon.
Dragon!

*With all the Predators absorbed, the Dragon exits. Small Fry
cautiously emerge from hiding.*

Small Fry 1   Oh my.

Small Fry 2   This is not good.

Small Fry 3   Money.

Small Fry 1   Magic numbers.

Small Fry 2   Dragons.

Small Fry 3   Not good at all.

They pick up the pot and are about to leave when Scavengers enter.

Scavenger *(astounded)* You got it?

Scavenger   I don't believe it.

Scavenger   You did it?

Scavenger   You got it back?

Scavenger   From Predators?

Small Fry 1   It's not what you think.

Small Fry 2   Not good.

Small Fry 3   Not good at all.

Scavenger   Not good for Predators, that's for sure!

Scavenger   Good for Scavengers though!

Small Fry 1   No. You don't understand –

Scavenger *(taking the pot)* Thanks very much.

Scavenger	You can clear off now.
Small Fry 2	Beg your pardon?
Scavenger	Clear off.
Scavenger	Back where you came from.
Small Fry 3	But ...
Scavengers *(all)*	Vanish!
Small Fry 1	But you said...
Small Fry 2	... we could
Small Fry 3	... stay.
Scavenger	Stay?
Small Fry 1	Bring back the Jackpot, you said
Small Fry 2	and we could stay
Small Fry 3	stay for good
Small Fry 1	with you
Small Fry 2	All be friends.

Scavengers fall about laughing.

Scavenger	Friends!
Scavenger	Stay for good!
Scavenger	With us!

Small Fry are dumbfounded.

Small Fry 3	You mean ...
Small Fry 1	... it wasn't true?

Small Fry 2	You were lying? (*Even more laughter.*)
Scavenger	What did you expect
Scavenger	in this place and time
Scavenger	this time and place?
Scavenger	What a scam!
Scavenger	What a dinker!
Scavenger	The perfect con!
Scavenger (*all*)	Hook, line and sinker!
Scavenger (*suddenly threatening*) Now clear off!	
Scavenger	Back where you came from!
Scavengers (*all*)	Vanish!

Scavengers chase Small Fry off and continue trying to get the lid off. But Small Fry return and watch from a hiding place.

Scavenger	Stuck.
Scavenger	Twist and prise with main and might
Scavenger	– it won't come off.
Scavenger	The lid's stuck tight.

Percussion announces the arrival of the Dragon.

Dragon	No point huffing and puffing
pulling and pushing.
Twist and prise with main and might
the lid of the pot
will stay on tight.

Scavenger	Who are you?
Dragon	Brute force will never succeed.
	To win the Jackpot a magic number is what you need.
Scavenger	Magic number?
Scavenger	What number?
Dragon	How much money?
Scavengers *(all)*	Money?
Dragon	In the pot. In the Jackpot. How much?
Scavenger *(hopeful)*	A hundred?
Dragon	More.
Scavenger	A thousand?
Dragon	Even more.
Scavenger	A million?!
Dragon	How many millions?
Scavenger	One?
Scavenger	Two?
Scavengers *(all)*	Three!

Instant percussion. During the following, the Dragon dances and whirls around the Scavengers weaving a spell which leaves them helpless to resist. One by one, they lose their identity and are absorbed into the Dragon.

Dragon	They think they're free to pick and choose but this is a game

of heads I win
and tails they lose.
I'll have them for breakfast
I'll swallow them whole
I'll chew on their flesh
And spit out their bones.
Neither human nor animal am I.
Neither living nor dead.
This place and time
this time and place
belong to me.
I am The Dragon.
Dragon!

Dragon exits. Small Fry cautiously emerge from hiding.

Small Fry 1   Oh my.

Small Fry 2   This is bad.

Small Fry 3   Very bad.

Small Fry 1   Money.

Small Fry 2   Magic numbers.

Small Fry 3   Dragons.

Small Fry 1   And nobody left.

Small Fry 2   Apart from us.

Small Fry 3   And the Jackpot.

Small Fry 1   Don't touch it!

Percussion. The Dragon enters.

Dragon   No point huffing and puffing
pulling and pushing
Twist and prise with main and might

the lid of the pot
will stay on tight.

Small Fry shrink away.

Small Fry 1   It can stay on tight

Small Fry 2   thank you very much.

Small Fry 3   We don't want it.

Dragon   Everyone wants money.
                         Lots of money
                         Pots of money
                         More than you've ever seen.
                         More than you've ever dreamed.

Small Fry 1   Don't need more

Small Fry 2   Thank you very much.

Small Fry 3   We have enough.

Dragon   No such thing as enough.
                         Everyone wants more.
                         More.
                         More.
                         More.
                         All you need
                         Is a magic number.

Small Fry 1   Don't know any magic numbers.

Dragon   It's easy.
                         Very easy.
                         How many are there of you?

Small Fry 2   Us?

Dragon   Small Fry.
                         How many Small Fry?
                         Count
                         Count

	Count.
Small Fry 3	No good at counting.
Small Fry 1	Hopeless at counting.
Small Fry 2	Can't count for toffee.

Dragon starts to lose patience with them.

Dragon	You have no choice.
	In this place and time
	this time and place
	there is no choice.
	Count!
	Unless you'd like me to swallow you whole,
	chew on your flesh
	and spit out your bones.
	Count!
	Count!
	Count!!

Small Fry 1 gingerly steps forward.

Small Fry 1 *(after much deliberation)* One?	
Dragon	Good.
	Very good...
	Didn't I tell you –
	it's easy.
	And the next...
Small Fry 1	... Two?
Dragon	Excellent!
	You see
	you can count
	And finally – last but not least ...

Small Fry 1	Me.
Dragon	Yes. But you have to count.
Small Fry 1	I did count.
Dragon	You didn't. You didn't count yourself.
Small Fry 1	I did.
Dragon	No you didn't.
Small Fry 1	I did. I'm sure I did.
Dragon	You didn't!
Small Fry 1	One ... Two ... and Me.
Dragon	That's not counting! You didn't count!
Small Fry 1	I told you we were no good at counting.
Dragon	What are you – an idiot?!
Small Fry 1	Sorry.

The Dragon gives up and turns to Small Fry 2.

Dragon	You! You try.
Small Fry 2	Me?
Dragon	Start with yourself. Think what number you are. Think hard. Now count.

Small Fry 2 *(hesitant)* One?

Dragon	Good. Someone with half a brain. Now the next.

Small Fry 2	Two?
Dragon	Fantastic! A born genius.
Dragon	Now this one the very last ...
Small Fry 2	Him?
Dragon	No! Not him!
Small Fry 2	Who?
Dragon	Not who!
Small Fry 2	I don't understand.
Dragon	Count! You have to count him!
Small Fry 2	I did count him.
Dragon	No you didn't!
Small Fry 2	I did. I'm sure I did.
Dragon	You didn't! You didn't count!
Small Fry 2	One ... Two ... and Him.

By now the Dragon is almost beside itself.

Dragon	But you have to say the number! You have to count! Idiots! You're all raving idiots!
Small Fry 3	I'm not! I'm not an idiot. I can do it. I can count. Let me try!
Dragon	Last one! Last chance! And this time, count!

Do you understand?
Count!
Start with him.

Small Fry 3 *(confident)* One.

Dragon   Keep going. Keep going.

Small Fry 3 *(very definite)* Two!

Dragon   At last, a mathematician.
Now
the big one.
The final one
Think hard.
Think carefully.
The very last Small Fry.
The final number ...

Small Fry 3   Her!

The Dragon explodes with rage.

Dragon   No! No! Not her! Not her!

Small Fry 3   Who?

Dragon   You have to count her!

Small Fry 3   I did count her!

Dragon   You didn't!
You didn't count!

Small Fry 3   I did! I definitely did!
One ... Two ... and Her!

Dragon   That's not counting!
You didn't count!
You didn't say the number!
You have to say the number!

Small Fry 3   What number?

Dragon	Three! One – two – three! You have to say the number three!!

Immediate percussion. Too late the Dragon realizes its mistake.

Dragon	No! Oh no! No!!

During the following, the Dragon dances and whirls around in chaotic fashion. Percussion and dance get faster and faster until the Dragon begins to come apart and break off into bits and pieces.

Dragon	I am the want that can never be met I am the hunger for more. I am the glut that is never enough I am the plenty of plenty I am the fever that poisons your mind I am the love of possession Neither human nor animal am I. Neither living nor dead. This place and time this time and place belong belong belong belong belong belong belong ...

Finally there is an explosion of percussion and the Dragon flies off in all directions. Predators and Scavengers begin to emerge – dazed and confused.

Predator	The Dragon –
Scavenger	Where's it gone?
Predator	Small Fry …
Scavenger	You?
Predator	Was it you?
Scavenger	Defeated the Dragon?
Predator	Rescued us?
Predators *(all)*	Predators.
Scavenger	Saved us?
Scavengers *(all)*	Scavengers.

Small Fry start to go.

Predator	Wait!
Scavenger	Where are you going?
Small Fry 1	Back.
Predator	Back?
Small Fry 2	Back where we came from.
Scavenger	Stop!
Predator	Can't just leave us!
Scavenger	Dragon might come back!
Predator	Have us for breakfast.
Predator	Swallow us whole.
Scavenger	Chew on our flesh
Scavenger	Spit out our bones.
Small Fry 3	Clear off, you said.
Small Fry 1	Back where you came from.

Small Fry *(all)*	Vanish!
Scavenger	You didn't believe us?
Predator	We weren't being serious.
Scavenger	It was a joke.
Predator	Just having a laugh.
Scavenger	Didn't mean it!
Predator	Never meant it!
Small Fry 2	Think you did.
Small Fry 3	It's best we leave.

They start to go again. Scavengers and Predators get panicky.

Scavenger	Alright!
Predator	Alright, we did mean it.
Scavenger	But we were wrong.
Predator	Dead wrong.
Scavenger	We're sorry.
Predator	Deeply sorry.
Scavenger	We apologise.
Predator	We want you to stay.
Scavenger	Stay for good.
Predator	With us.
Scavenger	All be friends.
Small Fry 3	Sorry.
Small Fry 1	Don't believe you.
Small Fry 2	Don't trust you.

Small Fry head off. Predators and Scavengers watch in despair. At the last moment Small Fry stop, think for a moment, exchange knowing glances.

Small Fry 3	There might ...
Small Fry 1	possibly...
Small Fry 2	be a way
Small Fry 1	for us to stay.
Scavenger	What is it?
Predator	Tell us.
Scavenger	We'll do whatever you say!
Small Fry 2	In this place and time
Small Fry 3	this time and place
Small Fry 1	rules are simple
Small Fry 2	rules are few.
Small Fry *(all)*	Rule one –
Small Fry 3	No snatching.
Small Fry 1	No grabbing.
Small Fry 2	No thieving.
Small Fry *(all)*	Rule two –
Small Fry 3	No lying.
Small Fry 1	No cheating.
Small Fry 2	No deceiving.
Small Fry *(all)*	Rule three –
Small Fry 3	Trust.
Scavengers/Predators *(all)* Trust?	
Small Fry 1	Trust your friends

Small Fry 2	Trust your brother
Small Fry 3	Trust your sister
Small Fry 1	Trust your mother
Small Fry *(all)*	Trust each other.
Scavenger	Even Predators?
Predator	Even Scavengers?
Small Fry 2	Trust.
Small Fry 3	Agreed?
Scavengers *(with some hesitance)* Agreed.	
Predators *(all)*	Agreed.
Scavenger	But what about the Jackpot?
Predator	Who gets to keep that?
Scavenger	It belongs to me.
Predator	No it doesn't.
Scavenger	It belongs to me.
Predator	It's mine!
Scavenger	It's mine!
Predator	Mine!
Scavenger	Mine!
Predator	Mine!
All	Mine!!

They immediately dissolve into a yelling and squabbling rabble. Small Fry cross over to the Jackpot, take off the lid, hold it open. The others stop and gaze in disbelief.

Predators	Empty?

Scavengers   Empty!

Small Fry laugh. And mimicking Scavengers' earlier lines...

Small Fry 1   What did you expect?

Small Fry 2   in this place and time

Small Fry 3   this time and place?

Small Fry 2   What a scam.

Small Fry 3   What a dinker.

Small Fry 1   The perfect con.

Small Fry *(all)*   Hook, line and sinker!

For a moment Scavengers and Predators are dumbfounded. Then gradually they begin to see the funny side and start to laugh. The laughter builds.

Percussion comes in. Small Fry begin to dance. They invite Predators and Scavengers to join them. Awkwardly and hesitantly they do so.

All three groups begin to dance. Happy, celebratory. A dance of togetherness.

All   In this place and time
this time and place
rules are simple
rules are few.
Rule one –
No snatching
No grabbing
No thieving
Rule two –
No lying
No cheating

No deceiving
Rule three –
Trust
Trust your friends.
Trust your brother.
Trust your sister.
Trust your mother.
Trust each other.
This place and time
This time and place
This place and time
This time and place
belong
belong
belong
belong
belong
belong
to US!!

They form an image of a place and time, a time and place, finally come together.

Lights down.
The end.

THE MINOTAUR

The Minotaur

What I like about the story of Theseus and the Minotaur is that it's not trapped in any historical time frame. It's a story for today. Its themes of war, conflict, jealousy, cycles of revenge, sibling rivalry, fears and nightmares are as much a part of our lives as they were thousands of years ago.

The gods are what we make them – thoughts, emotions, external pressures – they interfere in our lives, contradict one another, play with our destinies. But always we have a choice. We can heed what the gods say to us or we can ignore it. What the story teaches is that making choices is rarely easy. And we frequently make wrong ones.

In the research for the script I read many versions of the myth. By and large the play reflects these, but I've made one or two changes to give the story dramatic shape. The Greek myths tell us that Theseus and Daedalus were 'blood relations'. I exaggerated this to make them half-brothers and gave Daedalus a different reason for going to Crete to the one in the original myth.

Also, as most people will know, it was Icarus, Daedalus' son, who flew too near the sun and fell to his death. I changed this for reasons of simplicity. Icarus and Daedalus thus become one.

Finally there is the question of 'what is the Minotaur'? Again the myths provide different answers. Whatever version you choose it's clear that what Theseus has to face is his own worst nightmare, and it was this I chose to emphasise.

Facing up to our deepest fear is the hardest thing any of us ever do. In doing so Theseus becomes a hero. But heroes are far from perfect, as I hope the play manages to suggest.

THE MINOTAUR

Commissioned by Crucible Theatre, Sheffield. First performed at Crucible Theatre Studio on 21st February, 2004. Directed by Karen Simpson. Designed by Joslin McKinney. Composer Matthew Bugg.

CHARACTERS

Humans:

Theseus – a young warrior

Aethra – Theseus's mother

Daedalus – Theseus's half-brother *(played by a girl)*

Aegeus – Theseus's father. King of Athens

Medea – Aegeus's wife. Queen of Athens

Minos – King of Crete. Enemy of Aegeus

Ariadne – King Minos's daughter and Theseus's lover

Gods:

Apollo

Artemis

Aphrodite

Ares

Chorus – Numbers as required.

SET should be non-specific and multi-locational.

COSTUMES should be timeless with no attempt to fix the story in any historically accurate setting.

GODS wear half-masks. They are onstage throughout the play. When not involved in the action, they remain in the background observing what happens.

ACT ONE

Music in to underscore. Chorus fly a model seagull around the stage, causing it to swoop and glide as they speak.

Chorus	Beyond the realms of place and time
Chorus	lies a land where dreams are truth
Chorus	and truth is dreams,
Chorus	where the world of the flesh
Chorus	meets the world of the spirit.
Chorus	The name of this land is
Chorus	Myth.

They bring the seagull to rest somewhere on the set where it stays for the rest of the play. Ares enters.

Chorus	Ares!
Chorus	God of war.
Chorus	Terror and Fear are his weapons.
Chorus	Pain and Destruction follow his footsteps.
Chorus	The thrill of the fight.
Chorus	The pitch of battle.
Chorus	These are his loves.
Chorus	Death is his pleasure.

Aphrodite enters. She wears a silver cloth around her waist.

Chorus	Aphrodite.

Chorus	Goddess of love.
Chorus	Desire is the girdle which circles her waist.
Chorus	All who wear it become irresistible.
Chorus	The leap of love.
Chorus	The lure of passion.
Chorus	These are her spells.
Chorus	Temptation is her magic.

Artemis enters.

Chorus	Artemis.
Chorus	Goddess of vengeance.
Chorus	Justice is the bow she bends.
Chorus	Punishment, her arrows.
Chorus	Her target, all who transgress her code.
Chorus	Retribution is her duty.

Apollo enters.

Chorus	Apollo.
Chorus	God of culture.
Chorus imagination.	Music and art are the instruments of his
Chorus	Science and philosophy, the tools of his invention.
Chorus	Civilisation is his dream.
Chorus	These are the Gods of Olympus.
Chorus	The makers of heroes.

Chorus   The shapers of legend.

Chorus   The creators of Myth.

Chorus   Let the story begin …

Music ends. The Gods move into the background.
King Aegeus enters.

Chorus   After long years of war, King Aegeus is returning
   to his home in Athens

Chorus   where he has promised to marry the powerful
   Princess Medea.

Chorus   On the way, he stops for the night in the city of
   Troezen.

Aphrodite takes up the story.

Aphrodite   But there King Aegeus meets another princess...

Aethra enters.

Aphrodite   ... a princess whose beauty is as clear as the
   cloudless sky. (*She wraps her silver girdle around Aethra's waist.*)
   ... a princess who wears the girdle of Aphrodite.

Chorus   King Aegeus has never seen such a woman.

Chorus   Nor she such a man.

Aphrodite mischievously draws them towards each other.

Aegeus   But what of....

Aphrodite   Forget your betrothed. Think only of the woman who fills your thoughts.

Aegeus   But...

Aphrodite   Courage. Follow the yearnings of your heart. (*Gently and tenderly they begin to touch. Aphrodite enjoys her power over them.)* Have thoughts only for each other. And of the night ahead. (*They form an image of love. Aphrodite is delighted with her success.*)

Chorus   But when the night is gone and the grey light of morning dawns ...

Aphrodite removes the girdle from around Aethra's waist.

Chorus   King Aegeus sees his princess with different eyes.

Aegeus stares at Aethra.

Aethra   Why do you look at me that way?

Aegeus   There's something I should have told you.

Aphrodite   Why tell her now? Why cause her hurt?

Aethra   What is it?

Aegeus   I have to leave ... I have to return to Athens.

Aethra   Now? Not straight away?

Aegeus   I'll come back. It won't be for long, I promise.

Aethra   Stay. Please. If only for a while.

Aegeus   I'll come back for you, I swear.

Aethra   You promise?

Aphrodite   You're making things worse. Just go.

Aegeus(*drawing his sword*) I swear on my sword ... the sacred sword
   of Ares ... I place it here, beneath this rock. This is my vow to you,
   my promise to return.

Aegeus exits. Aethra remains on stage gazing after him.

Aethra   Is it true? Will he really come back?

Aphrodite   He gave his word.

Music in.

Chorus   Hours turn to days.

Chorus   And days to weeks.

*As Aethra waits for Aegeus's return, she strokes her pregnant
stomach.*

Aethra   When will he come?

Aphrodite   Soon. Very soon.

Aethra   It's been so long.

Music continues.

Chorus   Weeks turn to months.

Aphrodite folds up her cloth girdle to represent a baby.

Aethra   Will he ever come?

Aphrodite *(offering her the baby)* One day. One day he'll come.

Aethra *(takes the baby - which makes her very happy.)* I shall call him Theseus.

Aethra exits with the baby. Music ends.

Apollo	She has the right to know the truth.
Aphrodite	The truth would break her heart.
Apollo	She awaits a return that will never happen.
Aphrodite	You think she doesn't know that?

Apollo Why do you play these games? These are human lives.

Aphrodite I give them passion. I give them their heart's desire.

Apollo A mother with no husband? A child with no father? A king driven to lies and betrayal?

Artemis She shall be avenged for the wrong done to her.

Aphrodite Ah! I wondered when Artemis would start to meddle.

Artemis He deceived her. He deserted her.

Apollo And vengeance will only make things worse. There's nothing for you to do here.

Artemis You would deny a woman justice?

Apollo Revenge is not what she wants.

Artemis Aegeus did wrong, he must be punished.

Aphrodite And what sentence does the great Righter of Wrongs impose?

Artemis The day will come when Theseus will be bring about Aegeus's death.

Aphrodite   You'd have him kill his own father?!

Apollo   And who will gain from that? Not Theseus. Not his mother. What good is a punishment that changes nothing and helps no one?!

Artemis   I do what I do because it's right!

Artemis moves into the background.

Apollo *(to Aphrodite)* You see what your foolish games have set in motion. Where will all this end?

Apollo moves into the background. Music in. Aethra enters, singing to her baby. She stands gazing in the direction of Aegeus' leaving.

Aphrodite   One day he'll come. I promise you.

Aethra continues singing softly.

Chorus   Months turn to years.

Aphrodite gently takes the rolled up girdle from Aethra and goes into the background. Theseus appears as a young boy.

Chorus   Theseus grows into a fine strong boy.

Aethra watches the young Theseus at play.

Theseus   Mother ... Who is my father?

Aethra	When you're older. I'll tell you when you're older.
Chorus	And as the years pass, the boy grows into a youth.

Theseus 'grows'.

Theseus	Why does my father never come to see me?
Aethra	One day he will.
Theseus	How do you know?
Aethra	Aphrodite told me. The Goddess of Love gave me her promise.
Chorus	And finally the youth grows into a man.

Theseus 'grows' again. Music ends.

Theseus   I'm not a child any more. I have a right to know who my father is. (*Aethra hesitates, then approaches the rock and gently smoothes her hands across it.*)   What are you doing?

Aethra   If you've grown strong enough to move this rock, then I'll tell you.

Theseus approaches the rock. He uses all his strength to move it and finds the sword. He picks it up.

Aethra   It is the sword of Aegeus, King of Athens.

Theseus   Aegeus ...? Aegeus is my father?

Aethra   He placed it beneath this rock. It was his promise to me that he would return.

Theseus   Then I'll take it to him. I'll go to Athens and put it in his hand. I'll tell him to come back.

Aethra *(suddenly concerned)* You must never do that, Theseus. Never.

Theseus   But I have to tell him you're here – that you're still waiting.

Aethra   I don't want that. Don't you understand? Everything I want is here – with you.

Theseus   He left his sword. He gave his promise.

Aethra   And one day he'll come – of his own free will. I don't want to lose you.

Theseus   He's my father. I have to see him. I have to go.

Aethra   Please, Theseus ... don't do this. I beg you.

Theseus   It'll be alright, believe me ... I'll show him the sword. I'll tell him to send for you. You'll be with him again. We can live together – all of us – in Athens - as a family.

Theseus exits. Aethra watches sadly as he leaves in his father's footsteps. Aethra exits. Music link – time passing, different location. Theseus enters on his way to Athens. He stops to admire his sword. Tentatively tries it out – with no expertise whatsoever. Ares moves into the scene.

Ares   What are you? A girl?

Theseus stops, embarrassed at his lack of fighting skill.

Ares *(taking the sword)* This is the sword of Ares. It is intended for a warrior. *(Ares wields the sword with terrifying skill.)*

Theseus   How do you do that?

Ares *(handing back the sword)* Take it. *(Theseus tries to copy.)* You waft it around like a woman with a duster. It's a weapon. *(Theseus tries again – slightly better.)* Again. Faster. And this time shout.

Theseus	Shout?
Ares	At the top of your voice.
Theseus	What shall I shout?
Ares	You wish to be a warrior like your father?
Theseus	Yes.

Ares   Then shout. Terrify your enemy. (*Theseus tries.*) Louder! (*He tries again*) Louder still! Shout till your ears begin to split! (*Theseus manages to succeed.*)

Ares takes the sword and demonstrates sword movements.

Ares   Hack! Cut! Jab! Slash!

Theseus takes back the sword and copies, his aggression building.

Theseus	Hack! Cut! Jab! Slash!
Ares	Faster!
Theseus	Hack! Cut! Jab! Slash!
Ares	Faster still!
Theseus	Hack! Cut! Jab! Slash!
Ares	Now kill! Shout it – Kill!
Theseus	Kill! Kill! Kill! Kill!!

Theseus turns to Ares. Looks for a response.

Ares   Now you're beginning to look like a warrior. (*Ares moves into the background.*)

Theseus gazes at his sword, pleased and proud of himself. He exits.
Music link – time passing, different location.
Daedalus enters. He is a male character but played by a girl. He takes
the model of the seagull from the set and begins to work on it.
Theseus enters, sees Daedalus at work. His curiosity is aroused. He
watches for a few moments before making his presence known.

Theseus *(looking at the model)* That's good. It's very good.

Daedalus   Thank you.

Theseus   It almost looks alive.

Daedalus   They go where they please. Over white-capped
waves and mountains. Gliding like kites on the wind. They're my
dream.

Theseus   You dream of being a seagull?

Daedalus   I dream of having their wings. I dream of soaring
high above the clouds and over the ocean. Up there you can see
beyond the furthest horizon.

Theseus   What do you see?

Daedalus   Far in the distance I glimpse a gleaming kingdom.
A land of dreams. A land of the sun.

Theseus   What's it like, this land?

Daedalus   It's the most beautiful place on earth. I can see
palaces and temples. Columns of marble and walls of ashlar. Throne
rooms, shrines, schools, libraries, theatres. Statues of Apollo.
Painted frescoes – dolphins, lions, bulls – colours of gold and azure.
And everywhere there is light. Light and music – as dazzling as the
sky. I glimpse a world of joy, a world of sunlight... *(disturbed)* But
then ...

Theseus   Then what?

Daedalus   Then I want to see more. I want to fly higher. I
want to glimpse more of that world.

Theseus   And do you?

Daedalus   I fly higher. And higher still. The higher I fly the more I can see. I see children playing in the fields. I hear music – cool and vibrant. I want to fly higher, I want to see even more. But then something starts to happen. Something awful. Something terrifying.....

Theseus   What? What is it?

Daedalus   Something too horrible to speak of. Something so dreadful the very thought of it sets me shivering with terror. (*He stops, unable to continue.*)

Theseus   And then you wake. You wake up cold, your body wet with sweat. Your heart pounding like a drum. You peer into the darkness, gasping and shaking. You can't accept that the terror wasn't real. You can't believe it was only a nightmare.

Daedalus   ... You know.

Theseus   My dream is of a monster – it has the body of a man and the head and horns of a bull. It lives below the earth in a black maze of tunnels that has neither beginning nor end. I wander through those corridors filled with fear. I hear the monster bellowing in the dark. I sense its presence. Its stench fills my nostrils. Its foul breath surrounds me in the shadows. I start to run but my feet slip on the damp slime of the floor. The faster I run the more I slither and slide. I hear it pounding and roaring behind me. Fear wells up from my stomach. It fills my ears, my nose, my mouth. I try to scream but my voice is frozen. I slip, I stagger, I fall. I see its horns rising up above me, I feel the hot steam of its breath ... (*He stops.*)

Daedalus   And then you wake.

Theseus   Then I wake.

Pause.

Daedalus   What's your name?

Theseus   Theseus ... And yours?

Daedalus Daedalus.

Theseus *(surprised)* A boy? I took you for a girl.

Daedalus You sound like my father. He's always wanted me to be a warrior, the same as him.

Theseus My father's a warrior.

Daedalus What's his name?

Theseus Aegeus. King of Athens.

Daedalus *(astonished)* Aegeus?!

Theseus That's why I'm here. I've come to meet him. He's never seen me before. I'm not even sure he knows I exist.

Daedalus I'm absolutely certain he doesn't.

Theseus What do you mean?

Daedalus King Aegeus is my father too.

Theseus What?

Daedalus You and I are brothers.

Theseus No, it can't be. It's not true.

Daedalus We have the same father ... We're brothers!

Daedalus is delighted. Theseus is completely thrown.

Theseus Then who's your mother?

Daedalus Queen Medea.

Theseus He has a queen?

Daedalus Never in my wildest dreams did I imagine I had a brother!

Theseus He's married? He has a wife?

Daedalus I'll take you to meet them. We'll go straight away. Father won't be able to believe it!

He tries to go. Theseus holds back.

Daedalus   Come. We'll go together.

Theseus   No ... Not now ...

Daedalus   What's the matter? You came here to meet him ...
You're his son.

Theseus   You must never tell him that.

Daedalus   How can I not?

Theseus   Promise me .... You must never to tell my father
what I've told you.

Daedalus   But you're my brother!

Theseus   Promise me!

Daedalus   He needs to know!

Theseus   Promise!!

Pause. Daedalus sees that Theseus is in deadly earnest.

Daedalus   If that's what you wish then I shall say nothing.
What will you do?

Theseus   I need to think. I need time to think. *(He turns to
go.)*

Daedalus   Will I see you again?

*They gaze at each other for a moment. Theseus exits. Music link –
time passing, different location. Daedalus and Medea (his mother)
enter. Medea is very agitated. The two of them are in heated
conversation.*

Medea   Who is this boy? What's his name? How did you
meet him?!

Daedalus   His name is Theseus.

Medea   From here? Is he from Athens?!

Daedalus   No, mother. He's not from here.

Medea   Then where? Where *is* he from?

Daedalus   I don't know.

Medea   You don't know!

Daedalus   He didn't say.

Medea   I bet he didn't!

Daedalus   He's my brother!

Medea   So he claims ... And who is his mother?

Daedalus   I don't know.

Medea*(mimicking)* He didn't say.

Daedalus   I believe him. He's telling the truth.

Medea   You've never seen him before! You don't know who he is or where he comes from. Did he give you any proof of his ridiculous claims?

Daedalus   I didn't ask for any.

Medea   He's a charlatan. A confidence trickster. After money – or favours – or some position in court. I can't believe you were taken in by such blatant deception! (*Pause. She softens.*) You're too willing to see good in people. You always have been. There are bad people out there – people who are ready to tell lies and cheat their way into winning your friendship. I'm your mother – you have to trust me about such things.

Daedalus   He made me promise not to tell father.

Medea   And you mustn't. You must never breathe a word about this to him. Do you hear? Never.

Daedalus   But father would know. He'd be able to tell us the truth.

Medea   The truth is this Theseus of yours is a liar.

Put yourself in your father's place – how do you think he'd feel being accused of infidelity? He'd never forgive you. You must say nothing. Do you hear? Nothing.

King Aegeus enters.

Aegeus   Who must say nothing? What are you telling the boy to keep quiet about?

Medea quickly improvises.

Medea *(to Daedalus)* There you are! Didn't I tell you? I knew he'd find out!

Aegeus   Find out what?

Medea   Daedalus's secret. I've been trying my utmost to stop him telling you.

Aegeus   What secret? I'll have no secrets in my palace. *(to Daedalus)* Come on – out with it. What are you hiding?

Medea   It was meant to be a surprise. You weren't supposed to find out.

Aegeus   Find out what? Will the pair of you stop talking in riddles!

Medea   About his doll.

Aegeus   Doll?

Medea   Daedalus has made you a doll. He was going to give it you as a surprise – weren't you, Daedalus.

Aegeus   A doll?!

Medea   He invented it himself. *(to Daedalus)* Go and get it. Show your father.

Aegeus   My enemies are plotting against me, my kingdom is in the grip of a foreign tyrant and you think I have time to fritter away on dolls?!

Medea   It has moving arms and legs.

Aegeus   I don't care if it turns cartwheels and dances the syrtos, it's not dolls I need, it's warriors! Men who can fight! Can he give me them? Can he invent warriors? Warriors as good as this man Theseus!

Daedalus   Theseus?

Medea   You know of him?

Aegeus   Know of him? The whole of Athens knows of him. He's only won every event in the Olympic games. Give me a hundred like him and my troubles would be over. You should have seen his javelin. He threw it twice the distance of other competitors. The judges had to run for their lives. And his wrestling. He has the strength of a bull. He tossed Sinis clean out of the ring. What a champion! Why couldn't the Gods have blessed me with a son like him?! *(Pause.)*

Daedalus is deeply hurt. He stands stunned for a moment then exits.

Medea   You should not have said that to him.

Aegeus   Well, it's true. What use is a son who spends his life making models and playing the flute?

Medea   Our son is an artist.

Aegeus   Artists don't win wars.

Medea   Nor do they start them.

Aegeus   I need men with the strength and courage to stand up to King Minos.

Medea   And you think this Theseus is such a one?

Aegeus   With an army of soldiers like him, Minos would be finished.

Medea   More likely it would be you who were finished.

Aegeus   You're a woman. You have no knowledge of such things.

Medea   And what knowledge do you have? Do you know this Theseus? Do you know anything at all about him?

Aegeus   I know he's worth ten of any other.

Medea   Where is he from? What city? What nation? What is his parentage? His background?

Aegeus   How do I know? What does any of that matter?

Medea   Is it of no concern to you where his loyalties lie? Don't you think it matters what nationality he is – which side he belongs to?

Aegeus   What are you getting at?

Medea   Why has he come to Athens? What are his reasons? Does he have friends here? Family?

Aegeus   Not as far as I'm aware.

Medea   Then what are his motives? Has he offered any explanation?

Aegeus   He's an athlete – a warrior. He came to take part in the games.

Medea   But is that all? Can you be sure he has no hidden purpose? Something for which the games are merely a convenient cover.

Aegeus   You're not trying to suggest ...?

Medea   Warriors come from all over Greece to take part in the Olympics, even from Crete. Or have you forgotten the last time King Minos plotted against you?

Aegeus   You think he's an assassin? You think he's been sent to kill me?

Medea   Who would suspect a warrior who makes himself a champion in the eyes of all Athens?

Aegeus   It's true, I know nothing about this Theseus. No
one does. He's no family here – no connections. He simply
appeared. From nowhere. What am I do? I can't have him arrested.
There'd be uproar. He's made himself the hero of all Athens.

Medea   What did you do the last time you suspected such
a threat?

Aegeus   Poison?

Medea   Invite Theseus to the palace. Put on a feast to
celebrate his victory at the games. Then, at the height of the
festivities, he will be offered a goblet of wine.

*Music in – change of time and location. Music continues. Aegeus and
Medea reposition. Theseus enters, his sword carefully wrapped in a
cloth. He places it on the ground near to him. We're at the feast in
honour of Theseus's victory. Daedalus performs a delicate and
graceful dance. At the end of it, he bows and receives applause from
Medea and Theseus, and less enthusiastically from Aegeus.*

Aegeus   Perhaps our guest of honour would like to
demonstrate some of the skills for which he has become famed?

*Theseus bows. Music begins again. This time more aggressive.
Theseus does a very different dance – full of the images of battle.
Music ends. Daedalus, Medea, and Aegeus all applaud.*

Aegeus   Congratulations, Theseus. I see now why all
Athens regard you as their hero and champion.

*Aegeus throws a prompting look in Medea's direction. Medea picks up
a goblet. At the same time Theseus makes the decision to reveal the
sword to his father. He removes the cloth and places it on the ground
waiting for a response.*

Medea   After such an athletic performance our visitor needs wine to quench his thirst … Daedalus.

She hands the goblet to Daedalus who takes it to Theseus.

Daedalus *(offering the goblet)* You are as a brother to me.

Theseus takes the goblet, his attention still on Aegeus. He is on the point of drinking when Aegeus finally notices the sword.

Aegeus   Stop! Don't drink the wine!! That sword? Where did you get it? How did you come by it?

Theseus   It is from Troezen.

Aegeus *(shaking with emotion)* Troezen?

Theseus   The place of my birth. I took the sword from under a rock.

Aegeus   What rock? Tell me. How did you find it?

Theseus   My mother showed it to me. I took it from the same rock under which you placed it. It is the sacred sword of Ares. The sword which symbolised your promise to return.

Aegeus   My son …! You are my son! (*He embraces Theseus.*) You are my son! (*A moment of reunion.*)

Daedalus, who doesn't know about the poison, is as delighted as his father.

Daedalus(to Medea) You see. I told you he was my brother. I told you father would know the truth!

Too late Medea tries to shut Daedalus up. Aegeus hears the remark.
His mood changes instantly. He turns on Medea.

Aegeus   You knew ...? You knew he was my son? And yet
  you tried to make me poison him?!

Theseus   Poison?

Aegeus   The wine. It was meant to kill you. The two of
  them plotted to have me murder my own son!

Theseus immediately turns on Daedalus.

Daedalus   No! It's not true!

Theseus   As a brother to you, am I? A brother you would
  rather see dead!

Daedalus   I swear to you, Theseus, I didn't know!!

Theseus raises his sword to strike. Daedalus cowers under it. Pause.
Theseus stops himself, lowers the sword, turns away.

Aegeus   You are no longer my son. Nor you my wife. I
  disown you both. Leave my household and leave Athens and never
  shame me with your presence again.

Daedalus turns to leave.

Medea   Daedalus...

Daedalus rejects her and exits. Medea gives Aegeus a last, furious
glare.

Medea   You, not I, are the author of this tragedy.

She exits. Aegeus puts a fatherly arm around Theseus. They exit
together. Music link – change of time and location.
Daedalus enters. He carries a large travel sack and is alone.
Artemis moves into the scene.

Artemis   What thoughts now of your new-found brother?

Daedalus   He was going to kill me. I didn't know the wine
was poisoned. I had nothing to do with it. Why wouldn't he believe
me?

Artemis   Why wouldn't your father believe you?

Daedalus   My father hates me. I do everything I can to try
and please him. I make things, I dance, I play music for him, but he
hates me.

Artemis   And your mother?

Daedalus   My devoted, ever-loving mother ... She put the
cup in my hand. She tried to make me poison my own brother!

Artemis   And none of this angers you?

Daedalus   Of course it angers me. I feel let down. I feel
betrayed. I feel I want to get back at them all!

Artemis   Then do it. Do what you feel. Take your revenge.

Daedalus   How? You heard what father said – I'm a doll-
maker, a flute-player. How can someone like me get back at people
as powerful as them?

Artemis   Who is your father's greatest enemy?

Daedalus   What's that got to do with it?

Artemis   Who?

Daedalus   He sees enemies everywhere – most of them are
imaginary – in his head.

Artemis	But there is one who is not imaginary.
Daedalus	Minos?
Artemis	The most powerful ruler in all Greece.
Daedalus	You're not suggesting I go to King Minos? Father would never forgive me. He'd shut me out of his life for ever.
Artemis	Has he not done so already? Do you intend to remain a victim for the rest of your life? Or will you embark on the quest for justice?

Artemis moves into the background. Music in. Daedalus takes from his bag a model ship with twin white sails. He sails it through the air as a representation of his journey to the court of King Minos.

Chorus	So Daedalus sets sail from the land of his birth.
Chorus	Past the islands of Salamis and Idhra.
Chorus	Past the kingdoms of Serifos and Sifnos.
Chorus	Past Ios and Thira.
Chorus	Until finally he arrives at the home of the richest and most powerful ruler in all Greece.

Music ends. King Minos and his daughter Ariadne make a ceremonial entrance. Daedalus puts the model ship back in his bag and enters the scene.

Minos	What tangle of fate prompts the son of Aegeus to appear at the court of King Minos?
Daedalus	I am no longer the son of Aegeus.
Minos	Then there is discord in the state of Athens.
Daedalus	I've come to Crete to offer you my skills.
Minos	Skills? To your father's greatest enemy?

Daedalus   I am an artist and an inventor.

Daedalus reaches into his bag and produces a wooden doll with moving joints.

Ariadne *(delighted)* A doll! *(She takes it.)* It's beautiful. Look at it, father. Look at its eyes. They could be real – they look straight at you. And its legs – they move – just like ours! Its arms too! – You'd almost think it was alive!

Minos   Your work appears to have impressed my daughter.

Ariadne   What other things do you invent?

Daedalus   I came to your kingdom in a ship which has neither oars nor oarsmen.

Minos   Impossible. What would drive it forward? Such a ship would never cross the sea.

Daedalus reaches into his bag again and takes out the model ship with twin white sails.

Daedalus   I gave my ship wings – wings of cloth which billow in the breeze and send it speeding across the waves swifter than the pull of any oar.

Minos *(taking the model)* Wings? On a ship?

Daedalus   White and gleaming. Like the wings of a seagull. My ship lies at rest in your harbour. You will find no oars aboard it.

Minos *(impressed)* With a fleet of ships like this a king could rule the ocean.

Daedalus   And the wood to construct such a fleet – how would that be cut?

Minos   How else? With axes. Cretan axes are the sharpest
   in Greece.

Daedalus reaches into his bag and takes out a saw.

Daedalus   I have invented a tool with teeth as sharp as a
   crocodile's. It cuts through oak faster and straighter than a dozen
   Cretan axes.

Minos takes the saw. Tries his thumb against the teeth. Gets pricked.

Minos   Aegeus is more fool than I thought, to disown a
   son with such talent. Suppose I were to ask you to build me a
   palace ...

Daedalus   You would have a palace like no king before you.
   It would have columns of marble and walls of ashlar. Throne rooms,
   shrines, schools, libraries, theatres. Statues of Apollo. Painted
   frescoes – dolphins, lions, bulls – colours of gold and azure. And
   everywhere there would be light. Light and music. You would have a
   palace as dazzling as the sky. A palace of dreams. A palace of the
   sun.

Minos   And what would you expect in return for this
   palace of the sun?

Daedalus   I ask only for a place to live and the freedom to
   pursue my work.

Minos   Then you shall have it. You shall be given the best
   that Crete has to offer – workshops, materials, craftsmen,
   whatever you need – on one condition. Beneath this palace of the
   sun, you must build me another palace – a different palace.

Daedalus   What kind of palace?

Minos   Buried deep in the earth. A palace where no light
   shines and no music plays. I want you to build me a maze of tunnels

so complex and intertwined that no one who enters would ever emerge. A palace of the dark. A palace of fear. A labyrinth.

Daedalus   What purpose could such a terrible place serve?

Minos   That is not for you to know. There must be only one way out of this labyrinth. And you and I must be the only ones to share its secret. Do you agree? Do you give your solemn promise?

Daedalus   I will build your labyrinth and I swear to reveal its secret to no one but yourself.

They all exit. Music link – change of time and location.
We are back in Athens. Theseus enters, begins to work out.
Aegeus appears. His mood is downcast. The workout comes to an end.
Theseus looks to his father for acknowledgement.

Aegeus *(his mind on other things)* You are a son to make any father proud.

Theseus *(disappointed)* There is no greater warrior in all Greece.

Aegeus   Alas, the bravest are not always the most powerful.

Theseus   What's wrong? Is something the matter?

Aegeus *(deciding to tell him)* I have an enemy. The most powerful ruler on earth. His name is Minos. For years we fought to defend ourselves against him. But his armies are too strong... To prevent the destruction of our city, we were forced to agree to his demands.

Theseus   What are these demands?

Aegeus   Every year he sends a ship. We have to place aboard it seven young men and seven young women – the finest in Athens. They are taken away to Crete to live the rest of their lives as slaves.

Theseus   This is barbarous.

Aegeus   His ship lies in the harbour at this moment. It's a ship like no ocean has seen – with neither oars nor oarsmen. White cloth hangs from its mast like the wings of some giant bird. It is driven by the forces of sorcery.

Theseus　　　　　　　Send it back. Send back this ship of sorcery as empty as it came!

Aegeus　　　　　　　If only I were able. Minos would dispatch his armies to crush us. Athens would be destroyed.

Theseus　　　　　　　Then send me instead.

Aegeus　　　　　　　You?

Theseus　　　　　　　I'll go alone and confront this King Minos for the tyrant that he is.

Aegeus　　　　　　　He'd kill you without a moment's hesitation.

Theseus　　　　　　　I'm not afraid of a barbarian like him. I'll challenge him to single combat and set Athens free of his demands.

Aegeus　　　　　　　I can't let you to do that. You're my son, my only son.

Theseus　　　　　　　I'm a warrior. I shall kill this Minos and put an end to his reign of terror.

Aegeus　　　　　　　You don't know what he's like – he's a monster. I'd lose the only son I have.

Theseus *(drawing his sword)* I swear to you on the sacred sword of Ares – I shall rid you of this monster.

Aegeus　　　　　　　But how will I know? How will I know you've not been killed?

Theseus　　　　　　　That ship – that white winged ship that lies waiting in the harbour. On my return from Crete I'll pull down the white wings that hang from its mast and I'll hoist red ones instead. That will be the signal – to let you know I'm alive ... Keep a watch on the horizon. When you glimpse a far-off speck of red, you'll know that I've defeated Minos and I'm returning home in triumph.

Aegeus　　　　　　　But what if you lose? What if Minos kills you? What if the ship's wings are white?

Theseus   They won't be. They'll be red – the red of victory –
I promise you. Watch from the clifftop. Look out for the far-off
speck of red. The red wings will tell you I'm safe.

*They exit. Music in. Chorus sail the model ship through the air as they
speak.*

Chorus   The ship with neither oars nor oarsmen flies
Theseus like a seagull over the white-capped waves.

Chorus   Past the islands of Salamis and Idhra.

Chorus   Past the city of Troezen where an anxious mother
waits in vain for news of her son.

Chorus   Past the kingdoms of Serifos and Sifnos.

Chorus   Past Ios and Thira.

Chorus   Until finally it comes to rest in the harbour of the
richest and most powerful ruler in all Greece.

Theseus enters.

Chorus   Theseus goes at once to the palace of the sun.

Chorus   The palace built by his brother.

Chorus   But before he can confront Minos –

Chorus   – he meets Ariadne,

Chorus   daughter of Minos.

Ariadne enters. Aphrodite takes up the story.

Aphrodite   A princess whose beauty is as clear as the
cloudless sky. (*Aphrodite wraps her silver girdle around Ariadne's
waist.*) A princess who wears the girdle of Aphrodite …

Chorus   Theseus has never seen such a woman.

Chorus   Nor she such a man.

Aphrodite begins to draw them towards each other, once again enjoying her game.

Aphrodite   Have thoughts only for each other.

Theseus and Ariadne continue moving towards each other. They are about to embrace when Minos interrupts and they quickly separate. Annoyed, Aphrodite moves into the background. Music ends.

Minos   It is a brave messenger who dares to come to the court of King Minos with the news that Athens has failed to make the payment it owes.

Theseus   Only a tyrant would demand such a barbarous payment.

Minos   That's how they speak of me in Athens, is it?

Theseus   I've come here to challenge you to single combat – you or any champion you wish to name.

Minos   You're as hot-headed as you are brave. And if I refuse your challenge?

Theseus   Then you'll be known throughout Greece as a miserable coward.

Minos   As well as a barbarous tyrant?

Theseus   You mock me?

Minos   You mock yourself, my young warrior. The burden I impose on Athens is no more than justice demands.

Theseus   What sort of justice demands fourteen young men and women be taken every year as slaves?

Minos   Justice for the death of my son.

Theseus *(momentarily thrown)* Your son?

Minos   I see Aegeus failed to tell you about him. He was a warrior like yourself. He travelled to Athens in peace to take part in the games at Olympia. He swept all before him, winning every event. But Aegeus was convinced that my son had a different purpose – that he was an assassin sent by me to murder him. He put on a feast to celebrate my son's victory at the games. At the height of the festivities Aegeus offered him a goblet of wine.

Theseus   It's not true. Aegeus would never do such a terrible thing. I don't believe you!

Minos   Then you know the wine was poisoned?

Theseus   My father is not a murderer!

Minos *(surprised)* Your father?

Theseus   I am Theseus, son of Aegeus, and I don't believe a word of your lies!

Minos   So it appears that both Aegeus's sons have come to Crete.

Theseus   Daedalus…? Daedalus is here?

Minos   Your brother is a great artist. It was he who designed the ship that brought you here. And this palace – the palace of the sun.

Theseus   I should have killed him when I had the chance.

Minos   There is no love between you, I see.

Theseus   Daedalus is a coward and a traitor.

Minos   I've decided to accept your challenge, son of Aegeus. I will choose a champion to fight you. If you win, the payment from Athens will be ended. But if you lose – it will be doubled.

King Minos exits. Ariadne follows but quickly returns once her father is out of the way.

Ariadne   You must leave. Go at once. Leave Crete now!

Theseus   I can't do that. I came here to fight.

Ariadne   Fighting will achieve nothing. Please, Theseus.
Go. Before it's too late. Before you're hurt!

Theseus   I can't go back now. I have to do what I came for.
I have to defeat the tyrant.

Ariadne   My father's not a tyrant. What he's done to your
people is wrong, but he did it out of anger and grief over my
brother's death.

Theseus   You mean it's true?... Your brother was poisoned?

Ariadne   You must decide that for yourself. But don't you
see, you're making the same mistake as my father – vengeance
sparks only more vengeance. Fighting will lead to more fighting
and it will go on and on until no one knows how to stop.

Theseus   I can't give in now. People would think I ran
away. They'd say I was a coward like my brother.

Ariadne   Daedalus is not a coward, nor is he a traitor.
Believe me, Theseus, this is not the way... I'll go with you. We'll
leave together.

*She leads him off. Minos enters with Daedalus. Daedalus carries a
piece of pottery and is in a state of excitement.*

Daedalus   You place the clay on the wheel. You spin the
wheel. And you mould the vessel with your hands. It takes shape
before your eyes. It's so simple! Yet it produces the most perfectly-
shaped pottery. I can't understand why I never thought of it before.

Minos   Your inventions have provided me with
everything I asked for and more. But what of you? Are you happy
here in Crete? Don't you ever think of going home?

Daedalus   I can never go home.

Minos   You must sometimes get homesick. Don't you ever wish for news of your family – your mother and father?

Daedalus   My father disowned me. My mother tried to turn me into a murderer. As for my brother –

Minos *(feigning surprise)* You have a brother?

Daedalus   His name is Theseus. He's a great warrior. The sort of son my father always wanted.

Minos   Still, you must surely miss him. You must wonder where he is and what he's doing.

Daedalus   Last time I saw him he almost killed me.

Minos   His own brother?

Daedalus   They say he knows no fear – but I know he does.

Minos   All men know fear. Some merely refuse to admit it. What is it, this fear your brother has?

Daedalus   He has a nightmare. He dreams of a dreadful monster – half man, half bull.

Minos   Does he fight this monster? Does he defeat it?

Daedalus   He's helpless against it. He tries to run away but his legs refuse to move. He slips and falls. The monster towers over him.

Minos   And then?

Daedalus   Just as it's about to kill him – he wakes up. Cold and wet with perspiration. It's his worst horror.

Daedalus exits.

Minos   Half man, half bull ...

Minos exits, working on an idea. Ariadne enters with Theseus.

Ariadne   Once we're out of the palace we'll be safe. No one will see us. Your ship is waiting in the harbour.

Theseus   You want me to sneak away – like a thief in the night?

Ariadne   I want you to stay alive.

Minos enters unexpectedly.

Minos   Perhaps Ariadne has persuaded you to think better of your challenge. My daughter has always found it difficult to understand the necessity of conflict.

Ariadne   Will conflict restore my brother's life?

Minos   It will avenge his death.

Ariadne   I loved him as much as you did, but if we respond to his death by becoming killers ourselves then we dishonour his memory. Don't make revenge the excuse for Theseus to die.

Theseus   I need no one to plead for my life. I accept your terms. I'm ready to fight whatever champion you send against me.

Ariadne   Theseus, no!

Minos   Whatever champion I choose?

Theseus   Whoever you wish. I fear no one.

Minos   Then you will fight the Minotaur.

Ariadne   The Minotaur?

Minos   The champion I have chosen is neither man nor animal. It is a monster.

Ariadne   What kind of monster?

Minos   It has the body of a man, and the head and horns of a bull.

Theseus   … A bull?

Ariadne   Who could fight a beast like that? It will tear him to pieces. This isn't fair!

Minos   Was it fair for Aegeus to murder my son? You will fight the Minotaur in the dark maze of tunnels which lies beneath this palace. In the Labyrinth.

Theseus is visibly shaken.

Ariadne   How will he find his way out? He can't win! If he defeats the Minotaur he'll die an even more terrible death!

Minos   Theseus has a choice. He may withdraw his challenge, return to Athens, and inform his father that the payment to King Minos has been doubled.

Theseus   And suffer shame and disgrace forever. I'll enter your Labyrinth ... I'll face this Minotaur.

Theseus exits.

Ariadne *(calling after him)* Theseus! ... When is all this going to end?

Minos   When Aegeus feels the same hurt I feel.

Minos exits. Ariadne exits a moment later. Music link. Change of time and location. Daedalus enters, begins work on the model of the seagull. After a few moments, Ariadne enters.

Ariadne   Seagulls.

Daedalus   Neither kings nor slaves. They're the only ones who are truly free.

Ariadne   Free to fly to Athens?

Daedalus   I have no wish to do that.

Ariadne   Then fly somewhere else. Fly to a different place. Anywhere you please. And take Theseus with you.

Daedalus   Theseus?

Ariadne   Please Daedalus. Speak to him. Persuade him to leave. Take him with you away from here.

Daedalus   Theseus is here? In Crete?

Ariadne   Didn't my father tell you?

Daedalus   Why? What is he doing here?

Ariadne   He's issued a challenge. He has to go into the Labyrinth and fight my father's champion. But he can't win – the Minotaur is a monster. It has the body of a man and the head and horns of a bull.

Daedalus   His worst nightmare ... and I was the one to reveal it. Is there no one who can be trusted?! Is there not a single person I can confide in?!

Ariadne   You have to help him, Daedalus. He's terrified of this monster. I can see it in his eyes.

Daedalus   More terrified than you know. You must take him away from here before it's too late.

Ariadne   I've tried. He won't listen to me. You must persuade him.

Daedalus   I'm the last person on earth he'd listen to.

Ariadne   He's your brother. You can't just let him die! Please, Daedalus, you've got to help... Please!

Daedalus   You love him? (*Pause. Daedalus sees he's guessed right.*) Tell him this – that this champion of your father's – this Minotaur – is not as terrible as he imagines. It's not the awesome monster that haunts his dreams. It's not the nightmare that wakes him wet with terror. It's real. It's flesh and blood no different to his own. His greatest enemy is his own fear. His warrior skills will be useless. His sword will freeze in his hand. His legs will turn to jelly. Only by facing his fear will he survive. He must look the Minotaur in the eyes. He must seize hold of its horns. He must summon every ounce of strength in his body and pull the horns from its head! Only in this way can the Minotaur be defeated.

Ariadne But what about the Labyrinth? Even if he survives the Minotaur, how will he find his way out of the maze?

Daedalus ... That I'm not at liberty to tell.

Ariadne You built it. You know its secret. You know the way out!

Daedalus And I swore to your father I'd never reveal it.

Ariadne This is your brother. Would you have him die a slow and dreadful death in some dark corridor beneath your feet? Better he be torn to pieces by the Minotaur!

Daedalus I made a promise.

Ariadne And that's worth more than your brother's life?

Daedalus You must solve the problem of the Labyrinth yourself.

Ariadne How can I do that? How can anyone? ... Please, Daedalus.

Pause. Ariadne sees that Daedalus is torn.

Daedalus The Labyrinth is a tangle of tunnels. *(pointed)* It's a tangle that can be unwound.You must follow the thread of your thoughts.

Ariadne *(struggling to understand)* The thread of my thoughts ...? A tangle that can be unwound? I think I know what you're saying ... I think I understand! Oh thank you, Daedalus, thank you!

She gives him a hug and runs off. Daedalus returns to working on his model. Theseus enters.

Theseus   Still trying to glimpse gleaming kingdoms? Still wishing you could fly?

Daedalus *(cautious)* Perhaps one day I will.

Theseus   You're a dreamer, Daedalus.

Daedalus   Is that a bad thing?

Theseus   Not as bad as being a traitor.

Daedalus   I'm not sure I know what being a traitor means.

Theseus   It means betraying your own people.

Daedalus   Who are my people, Theseus?

Pause. Theseus softens.

Theseus   If I don't see you again ...

Daedalus   We're brothers. Neither of us is able to change that.

Daedalus exits. Theseus is left alone for a moment.
Ariadne runs in carrying a ball of twine, expecting to see Daedalus.

Ariadne   Theseus ... I thought Daedalus was here.

Theseus   He just left.

Ariadne   We still have time. Your ship's in the harbour. There'd be no shame, no disgrace. You have no chance against this bull monster.

For a second Theseus is almost tempted.

Theseus   I promised my father.

Ariadne   ... Then you won't go alone.

Theseus   What?

Ariadne   I'm coming with you.

Theseus   Are you mad? The Minotaur would kill you as readily as it will me.

Ariadne   Then we'll face it together.

Theseus   This is not your fight.

Ariadne   Nor is it yours. It's between our fathers.

Theseus   I have to face the Minotaur alone.

Ariadne   And if you win? How will you find your way out of the Labyrinth?

Theseus   I'll cross that bridge when I come to it.

Ariadne   I can show you the way.

Theseus   You?

Ariadne   Come. We'll enter together.
(*She ties the end of the twine to a point on the set.*)
(*To herself*) Follow the thread of your thoughts ...

They approach the entrance to the Labyrinth. Music/percussion in.
Theseus holds back.

Theseus   This is my nightmare. This is the black maze of tunnels that haunts my dreams.

Ariadne   Courage.

They enter the Labyrinth. Music begins softly and gradually builds throughout their journey. Ariadne unwinds the twine as they proceed. Every step increases Theseus's dread. Every sound fills him with horror. We hear a deep musical roar.

| **Theseus** | Listen ... The Minotaur. I can hear it bellowing! |
| **Ariadne** | It's just an echo – an echo in the corridors. |

Be strong.

They continue on as the underscoring builds. Another musical roar.
This time louder.

| **Theseus** | There it is again!! |
| **Ariadne** | It's your own fear. Don't let it overcome you. |

They continue on through the maze. We hear a musical breathing.

Theseus   There – lurking in the dark! I can hear its
breathing! (*The musical breathing builds. Theseus begins to panic.*)
Its stench fills my nostrils. Its foul breath surrounds me in the
shadows!

Ariadne   It's not what you think. It's not the monster of
your dreams!

Theseus   I can hear its roar. I feel its presence!
(*Music builds to a climax.*) It's here! It's coming!
(*He starts to run but he slips and falls.*)

Ariadne	Face it, Theseus! You must face it!
Theseus	I can hear it pounding and roaring behind me!
Ariadne	You have to face it, Theseus! Look it the eye!

Theseus runs away again. He falls. Music reaches a crescendo.
Suddenly the Minotaur appears in front of him – huge and terrifying.
Music hangs in the air. Theseus turns away in terror.

| **Theseus** | It fills my ears, my nose, my mouth. |

Ariadne   Face it, Theseus! Look it in the eye! You have to face it!

Theseus   I see its horns rising up above me. I feel the hot steam of its breath ...

Ariadne   Wake up, Theseus! You must wake up! (*She pulls Theseus out of his trance.*) It's not the monster of your dreams! It's real! It's flesh and blood – no different to your own!... Face it, Theseus! Look it in the eye!

Theseus turns to confront the Minotaur. The Minotaur hesitates, starts to back away.

Ariadne   You see. It's real. It's alive. It knows fear – the same as you! (*Theseus starts to move forward.*) Take hold of its horns! Seize it by the horns! (*Theseus grabs the Minotaur by the horns.*) Pull them off! Summon all your strength! Pull off the Minotaur's horns!

They begin to wrestle. Theseus's confidence begins to grow. He begins to gain the upper hand. Finally with a mighty pull on the Minotaur's horns, the whole bull's head comes away – revealing King Minos. Music/percussion ends.

Theseus   Minos?! You are the Minotaur? The creature that's haunted my dreams? Then I'll put an end to this nightmare for good! (*He raises his sword intending to kill Minos.*)

Ariadne   Theseus!

Theseus stops. A pause. Ariadne looks on in horror. Finally, Theseus places his sword on the ground in front of Minos and steps back.

Theseus   Let this be an end. An end to it all.

Minos gathers himself together, picks up Theseus' sword and the Minotaur mask.

Ariadne   Father ...

Minos   You are no longer my daughter. Stay with your lover. Stay with him forever ... in the Labyrinth.

Minos exits, taking Theseus's sword with him. A pause.

Theseus   You've lost everything because of me.

Ariadne   Not everything. The Labyrinth is a tangle that can be unwound. We must follow the thread of our thoughts.

Theseus   The twine?

Ariadne   Daedalus is the one you must thank. Without his help neither of us would see the sun again.

She starts to wind up the twine. Eventually it leads them back to the entrance of the Labyrinth.

Theseus   Is that ship still in the harbour?

Ariadne   Still waiting.

Theseus   Then let's take it. Let's fly away. You and I.

Ariadne   Where to?

Theseus   To a land beyond the furthest ocean. To a gleaming kingdom glimpsed only by seagulls.

Ariadne   You sound like your brother.

Theseus   Is that a bad thing?

They both exit. Music link – change of time and location. Minos enters.
He paces up and down impatiently. Daedalus enters in chains.

Daedalus   Is this your doing? I was dragged out of my house.
I was brought here under armed guard!

Minos   You're lucky I didn't have you put to death on the
spot. You gave your word. You made a solemn vow never to reveal
the secret of the Labyrinth!

Daedalus   And I've kept that vow.

Minos   So how is it your brother managed to find his way
out and escape from Crete, taking my daughter with him?!

Daedalus   They've gone?

Minos   And you helped them. You told them the secret!

Daedalus   I told them nothing. Your daughter is cleverer
than you think. She must have unravelled the secret of the Labyrinth
herself.

Minos   You're lying. You broke your promise – you
betrayed the trust I placed in you. For that you'll be imprisoned at
the top of the highest tower in Crete. You'll see no one and speak to
no one. And you'll stay there till you rot.

Minos exits. Daedalus exits. Music link – change of time and location.
Theseus and Ariadne enter. They have just landed on a remote island
and are gazing round at their new surroundings. They're clearly very
much in love.

Ariadne   Where are we?

Theseus   This is the place. This is the kingdom glimpsed
only by seagulls.

Ariadne   Does anyone live here?

Theseus   No one. We're the first. The past holds no power
here.

Ariadne   Then we can make of it whatever we like.

Theseus   Anything we wish.

Ariadne   No wars. No more quests for vengeance.

Theseus   Our fathers will never find us here.

Ariadne   We'll build the most beautiful kingdom on earth –
a land of laughter and children.

Theseus   No monsters.

Ariadne   No Minotaurs. No dark nightmares.
No Labyrinths.

Theseus   No Cretans or Athenians.

Ariadne   A land of dreams.

Theseus   The land of the sun.

*They lie down in each other's arms and sleep. They remain there while
Daedalus enters on a separate part of the acting area. He's
imprisoned in the tower. Apollo moves into the scene.*

Daedalus   Was Minos right? Did I betray the trust he placed
in me?

Apollo   Only you know that.

Daedalus   How do you choose between a promise made to a
king and the life of your own brother?

Apollo   Choosing which path to follow is never simple –
even for a maze builder.

Daedalus   But there are right paths and wrong paths
even in a maze.

Apollo   Right for whom? For Minos? For Theseus?
For your father?

Daedalus   I tried to do what I thought was right for all of
them.

Apollo   Then maybe you should try to do what you think
is right for yourself.

Daedalus   I'm in prison. I'm locked at the top of the highest
tower in all Crete!

Apollo   Then escape.

Daedalus   Oh fine. Why didn't I think of it? Jump out of the
window shall I? Soar like a seagull over the rooftops?

Apollo   Why not?

Daedalus   Perhaps you haven't noticed – I don't happen to
have wings.

Apollo   Then invent them.

Daedalus   Invent them?

Apollo   You invented them for ships. Who knows more
than you how a bird flies? You've studied their movement, their
anatomy, the pattern of their flight. You know everything about
them.

Daedalus   I've no tools, no materials.

Apollo produces a couple of feathers.

Apollo   Seagulls perch on your window ledge. They nest
on your roof. Their feathers are all around.

Daedalus *(taking the feathers)* How would I fasten them together?
What would hold them to my arms?

Apollo   What lights your room at night?

Daedalus   Candle wax! I could fix them with candle wax!

Apollo   Then spread you wings and fly high over the
rooftops. Above the clouds and over the ocean.

Daedalus   Towards the far-distant horizon.

Apollo   The land of the sun.

Daedalus   I'll do it. Make wings. I'll escape from this prison.
And fly to the land of the sun!

*Music link as Daedalus exits. Apollo moves into the background.
Focus shifts back to the other part of the acting area where Theseus
and Ariadne are still sleeping. Ares and Aphrodite move into the
action. Ares carries Theseus' sword. They stand watching the sleeping
couple. A silent pact is made between them.*

Aphrodite   When the night is gone and the grey light of
morning dawns ... *(Aphrodite gently removes her girdle from
around Ariadne's waist.)* Theseus sees his princess with different
eyes.

*Aphrodite moves into the background. Theseus begins to wake.
Ariadne sleeps on. He stares at her.*

Ares   Look carefully. Is she as beautiful as you thought?
Is she worth the sacrifice. What is this place you've come to? What
will you do here? How will you spend your days? Play music?
Dance? You're a warrior.

Theseus   I can change. I can become something else.

Ares   What will you become? A dreamer? Like your
brother – more woman than man? Perhaps you can learn to make
dolls.

Theseus   She saved my life.

Ares   And now she's taking it away from you. Do you want to live your life surrounded by the virtuous and the weak? Have you forgotten the rush of blood, the thrill of the fight? You're the warrior who defeated Minos – the greatest champion Athens has ever known.

Theseus   We could go back. I could take her home with me to Athens.

Ares   A Cretan? The daughter of your father's most hated enemy? What sort of welcome would you receive? No victory parades, no celebrations. People would turn their backs, and with good reason. An Athenian married to a Cretan?

Theseus   I can't leave her here.

Ares   What else can you do? Take her back to Crete? Minos would kill you both. Take her with you to Athens? She'd be hated and reviled and you'd be an outcast – no better than your brother. *(offering Theseus his sword)* Leave now. Before she wakes. No tears. No good byes. *(Theseus is torn.)* There's no other way and you know it. Go home. Enjoy the triumph of your victory.

Theseus hesitates a moment or two longer, then takes the sword and exits. Music link. Ares and Aphrodite enjoy their success.
Focus moves back to the other part of the acting area. Daedalus enters with large white wings attached to his arms. Apollo enters the scene.

Apollo   Stand on the window sill.

Daedalus does so. He looks down.

Daedalus   What if I –?

Apollo   You won't ... You'll soar into the sky like a seagull. Open up your wings.

Daedalus   I can feel the breeze. I can feel it lifting me!

Apollo   Let it. Let it fill your wings as it fills the sails of
   your ship.

Daedalus   It's strong. It's so strong.

Apollo   Trust in it. Give yourself to it. Do what you've
   always dreamed of – Fly!

*Music in. Daedalus spreads his wings. Chorus gently lift him into the
air.*

Daedalus   It works! I'm flying! Like a bird! I'm flying!!

Chorus   High over the rooftops.

Chorus   Like a seagull on the breeze.

Daedalus   I can see the palace I built for Minos. Roofs,
   columns, statues, painted walls.

Apollo   Look beyond it. What else do you see?

Daedalus   The sea. Blue and shimmering. Wrapping the
   earth in a huge arc. I want to fly higher. I want to see more!

Apollo   Look further. Look towards the far horizon.

Daedalus   I see the sky and the sea becoming one. I want to
   fly higher. I want to see more!

Apollo   Then fly higher. Fly as high as you can. Away from
   Crete. Away from Athens. Fly beyond the furthest horizon!

Music builds as the Chorus carry Daedalus offstage.
Apollo returns to the background. Music ends.
Elsewhere (back on the island), Ariadne begins to awaken.

Ariadne   Theseus ... Theseus?

She gets up. Searches round for him.

Ariadne   Theseus, where are you!

Artemis moves into the scene.

Artemis   Your lover is gone.

Ariadne   Gone?

Artemis   Deserted you. As men have always done.

Ariadne   I don't believe you. *(She searches round some more.)* Theseus! Theseus!

Artemis   Theseus is gone. He has left you.

Ariadne continues frantically searching until she eventually gives up in despair.

Artemis   How could he do this to me? Is that what you're thinking? After all we said to one another. After all the vows we made. How could he leave with not even a word?

Ariadne   We were to build a land of dreams – a land born of love.

Artemis   Now you must build it alone.

Ariadne   He brought me here. This was his gleaming kingdom, his land of the sun.

Artemis   He won't go unpunished. You shall be avenged.

Ariadne   Avenged?

Artemis   See for yourself how fate resolves this tale of human frailty.

*Artemis leads Ariadne to a point on the set where they can watch
what happens. Music in. In the following the Chorus is split into three
sections. Chorus 1 enter with the model ship, making it sail through
the air. Theseus accompanies them, as if sailing on the ship.*

Artemis   Theseus – your fickle and faithless lover –
returning to Athens on the ship made by his brother.
(Chorus 2 enter carrying Aegeus.)
His father, King Aegeus – equally fickle and faithless – stands high
on the cliffs over Athens. Scanning the horizon for his son's return.

Aegeus   I see a shape. A speck on the horizon. Is it a
cloud...? Or a ship?

Artemis   His eyes are old. His sight is dim.

Theseus   I see the land, green and welcoming. I see the
gleaming city of Athens. I see the cliffs, rising above it.

Aegeus   A ship. It's a ship!

Artemis   Could it be his son? Could it be Theseus returning
home?

Theseus   I see my father! He's standing on the cliffs. He's
looking out for me. He's waiting to welcome me home!

Artemis   But in his thirst for glory, your lover has forgotten
the promise he made.

Aegeus   The signal. The wings that hang from the ship's
mast. Are they white – or are they red?

Artemis   Let the bow of justice be bent! Let the arrows of
retribution find their mark!

Ariadne   No! I don't want that! Don't let it happen!

Theseus   Father! I'm here! It's Theseus! I fought the
Minotaur! I defeated King Minos!

Aegeus   White ...! The wings on the ship are white! –
My son is dead!

Music in. Chorus 3 enter carrying Daedalus. His wings spread wide. We now have four scenes happening at once and in different areas of the stage:

Theseus on board the ship /

Aegeus on top of the cliff /

Daedalus flying /

And Ariadne and Artemis watching it all.

Daedalus   High over the sea I fly! Higher and higher! *(He suddenly starts to wobble.)* What's happening?... I feel the sun warm on my back. I feel its heat, its glow. My wings. The wax is starting to melt!

Elsewhere on the set, Aegeus opens out his arms as if to jump from the cliff.

Theseus   I see my father stretching out his arms like a seagull.

Aegeus   Theseus!

Theseus   I see him leap from the cliff. *(Chorus slowly and gently simulate Aegeus's fall.)* I see him falling!

Daedalus   I see feathers swirling around me. *(In almost a mirror image Chorus simulate Daedalus's fall.)* I see the earth speeding up to meet me. This is my dream! This is my nightmare!!

Theseus   Father!!!

Theseus collapses as Aegeus and Daedalus are both carried off stage by the Chorus.

Music ends. Chorus exit leaving behind the model ship, Daedalus' wings, and Aegeus' crown.

Ariadne wanders through the detritus.

Ariadne   Aegeus and Daedalus dead. Lives torn asunder...
  Why? For what reason?

Artemis   For justice. Wrongs must be avenged.

Ariadne   But what has it achieved? What good has come of
  it?

Ares moves into the scene.

Ares   The name of Theseus will live forever. The
  greatest warrior in all Greece. The hero who conquered the
  Minotaur.

Ariadne   And what of those who are left behind? Those
  who have to find a way out of this tangled maze? What do the Gods
  have planned for us?

Music in. Aphrodite and Apollo move into the scene. Apollo takes the model seagull from the set and offers it to Ariadne – a symbol of hope. She gazes at it for a moment. Takes it. The music builds.

Chorus   Beyond the realms of place and time,

Chorus   exists a land where dreams are truth

Chorus   and truth is dreams,

Chorus   where the world of the flesh

Chorus   meets the world of the spirit.

Ariadne holds out the seagull as if offering it to the audience.

Chorus   The name of this land is –

Chorus *(all)*   Myth.

Music ends.

Lights down.
The end.

TALKING WITH ANGELS

Talking with Angels

What becomes apparent, almost as you start reading about Joan of Arc, is that the real Joan – the teenager who first heard voices in the fields of Domremy – has been irretrievably lost, buried forever in the legend that grew up around her. Virtually every account we read – what she did, what she said, how she behaved, what her motivations were – has been shaped and moulded to suit the interests of whoever happens to be telling the story at the time. Saint, prophet, witch, warrior, virgin, whore, princess, peasant, heroine, heretic, martyr, nationalist, revolutionary – Joan has been all these and more.

What we do know is that she was an extraordinary young woman. In the space of less than a year, she propelled herself from unknown shepherd girl to French national heroine, scourge of the English and famed throughout Europe – a danger not only to the English invader but also to the established church and sections of the French social order. Joan was executed not because of what she did but because of what she represented – what she inspired in others.

She was capable of extraordinary courage and bravery, yet filled with the fear (as we all are) of physical pain and death. Humbly born, she refused to be intimidated by wealth and nobility. Barely educated, yet capable of holding her own against professional lawyers. A devout Christian, and at the same time, an uncompromising warmonger. A teenage girl in a world controlled by men, who battled both insult and prejudice against her sex, and insisted until her death on the right to dress in the clothes of a man.

It seems to me that the voices Joan heard were unquestionably real to her. She believed in them completely. For her, they were exactly what they claimed to be – angels from heaven, messengers from God. I find it inconceivable that she could have been lying about them. Whatever the voices were, to Joan they were real and she felt impelled to obey them.

What this incredible teenager managed to achieve in the space of less than two years makes for one of the most astounding stories in history.

TALKING WITH ANGELS

Commissioned and first performed by Quicksilver Theatre at Trinity Arts Centre, Tunbridge Wells on 7th october, 2001. Directed by Guy Holland. Designed by Philip Englheart. Composer Steve Byrne.

CHARACTERS

Joan – a teenager

Uncle – Joan's uncle.

Prince – Prince of the Whites.

Duke (white)

English Soldier (blue)

White Soldier

Red Soldier

Blue Soldier

English Commander (blue)

Voices (several)

Captain of the Guard (white)

Gatekeeper (white)

English Noble (blue)

Red Lawyers 1 & 2

Scribe (neutral)

Peasant Woman (neutral)

MUSIC: can be used wherever possible to underscore and punctuate the action, to create atmosphere, and signal shifts in time and location.
SET: should be non-specific and should be able to represent many different locations.
COSTUME: Colour of costume should indicate the character's political allegiance (white, red, blue or neutral).

ACT ONE

Music. Lights up on the Voices. They wear white and gold half-masks.

Voice	The time is long ago.
Voice	The place is France.
Voice	The nation is at war with itself.

Dramatic percussion. Two soldiers enter one dressed in white, the other red. They carry weapons and confront each other as enemies.

White Soldier	On one side are the Whites.
Red Soldier	On the other – the Reds.

The two soldiers attack each other. A fierce stylised combat with percussion accompaniment.

Voice	Homes looted!
Voice	Houses burned!
Voice	Towns and villages destroyed!
Voice	Innocent people slaughtered!
Soldiers	All the fault of the Whites/Reds!

The battle continues.

Voice	The fighting goes on for years.
Voice	Neither side able to defeat the other.

The White Soldier begins to get on top.

White Soldier   Until finally the Whites gain the advantage!

Soldiers freeze – the Red Soldier's defences are down, the White Soldier is about to strike the fatal blow. Percussion softens. A third soldier arrives wearing blue.

Voice   But just when all seems lost,

Voice   a messenger arrives

Voice   from across the sea.

Blue Soldier approaches the Red Soldier who remains in freeze – about to be killed.

Blue Soldier   The King of England sends you his greetings.

Red Soldier *(more concerned about dying)* Very thoughtful of him.

Blue Soldier   He offers help.

Red Soldier   Help?

Blue Soldier   He's willing to send his army to fight on your side.

Red Soldier   The English army?... But that's wonderful. Tell him yes – tell him thank you – as soon as possible!

Blue Soldier   On one condition ...

Red Soldier   Name it. He can have whatever he wants.

Blue Soldier   When the war is over, the King of England must also become King of France.

Red Soldier   That's not right. He can't be king of two countries.

Blue Soldier *(to the White Soldier)* Looks to me like you don't have much choice.

Voice   The Reds have to think hard and long.

Blue Soldier *(insistent)* But not too long.

Red Soldier *(hesitates)* Agreed.

Percussion swells again. Soldiers break the freeze.

Voice   So the English army arrives in France.

Voice   To fight alongside the Reds.

Blue and Red Soldiers confront the White Soldier. Battle resumes.
The White Soldier is gradually forced back.

Red Soldier   Now who's got the advantage?!

Percussion stops. Soldiers freeze with the previous positions reversed,
the White Soldier now facing defeat.
Joan appears. She wears a white cloth tied around her waist like a
skirt and carries a skipping rope. Initially, we see her as child-like and
vulnerable, not at all sure of herself. She picks her way warily through
the soldiers' freeze, very much conscious of what it represents.

Voice   At the heart of the fighting lies a village.

Voice   In the village lives a girl.

Voice   Her name is Joan.

The three soldiers break their freeze and exit. Music in.
Joan starts to skip and sing.

Joan   Here am I
                     Little jumping Joan
                     When nobody's with me
                     I'm all alone *(A Voice joins in.)*

Joan/Voice   Here am I
                     Little jumping Joan

When nobody's with me
I'm all alone.
(The other Voices join in.)

Joan/Voices   Here am I
Little jumping Joan
When nobody's with me
I'm all alone

Joan stops skipping. Voices move towards her. She senses her voices rather than merely hearing them. Though not strictly seeing them, she always knows where they are and on occasion may look at and talk to them directly.

Voice   But Joan is not alone.

Voice   She has her Voices.

Voice   Sometimes one.

Voice   Sometimes more.

Voice   Voices no one else can hear.

Joan   Who are you? Why do you keep coming to me?

Voice   They whisper to her from the leaves of the tree.

Voice   They sing to her from the brook.

Voice   They ring out from the angelus bell in the village church.

Joan   Do other people hear you? Is it only me you speak to?

Sudden percussion interrupts. Harsh and violent. A Blue Soldier appears carrying a blue flag.

Voice   One day English soldiers come to Joan's village.

*Percussion continues. Joan starts to back away. Her voices remain
though the soldier is unaware of them. They watch and react to what
happens. The soldier advances on Joan. She finds herself cornered. He
tears the skipping rope away from her. Joan is terrified. He pulls the
white cloth from around her waist, shoves the blue flag at her.*

Blue Soldier   Put it on. *(Joan hesitates, glances at her Voices.)*
  Put it on! *(She ties the flag around her waist. The soldier thrusts
  the rope at her.)* Now skip.

*Scared out of her wits, Joan takes the rope and starts to skip. Finally
satisfied, the soldier exits. Percussion ends. Joan continues skipping
until she feels it's safe to stop. She stands in silence, too frightened to
move. Music in to underscore.*

Voice	Why do they come here?
Voice	This is our village.
Voice	Our land.
Voice	France belongs to the French.
Voice	Not the English.
Voice	They have no right.
Joan	They do whatever they like. They're too strong.
Voice	Killing.
Voice	Stealing.
Voice	Burning.
Voice	It shouldn't be allowed.
Voice	Someone ought to stop them.
Joan	It's no good. People have tried. No one can stop them.
Voice	Then *you* must.

Joan	... Me?
Voice	*You* must stop them.
Joan	Are you mad – they're soldiers – English soldiers – what can *I* do?
Voice	It has to end.
Voice	They must be driven out.
Joan	I can't do that!
Voice	There is no one else.

The Voices take hold of the blue cloth around her waist.

Voice	This cloth is a sign.
Voice	A sign that you have been chosen.
Voice	To drive out the English.

They pull the blue cloth from her waist and toss it away.

Joan	But who's chosen me? And why? Why me?
Voice	You must believe in yourself.
Voice	Trust in your voices.
Joan	I'm just a girl.
Voice	A maid.
Voice	A young village maid.

They tie the white cloth back around her waist.

Joan   Like the maid in the prophecy? Is that what you're
saying? I'm the maid in the prophecy?

Voice   You must leave at once.

Voice   Go to the Prince of the Whites.

Voice   Tell him to put you in charge of his army.

Joan   They'd think I was mad – they'd all laugh at me!

Voice   Believe in yourself.

Joan   Who are you? Where do you come from?

Voice   We are your voices.

Joan   Inside my head – is that where you are?

Voice   We are your voices.

Joan (*suddenly frightened*) You're not ghosts are you? Or demons?

*They begin to turn the skipping rope, calmly waiting for her to jump
in.*

Joan   No. No you're not demons – you're too good, too
kind... I know who you are. (*They continue turning the rope,
waiting.*) You've come from God, haven't you? This is a message
from Him. This is what God wants me to do. (*They continue
turning. She becomes more convinced.*) You're angels, aren't you?
That's who you are ... You're God's holy angels.

*They continue turning. Now certain she now knows who they are,
Joan jumps in and starts to skip and sing.*

Joan   Here am I
                        Little jumping Joan
                        When nobody's with me
                        I'm not alone.
                        (*Voices join in.*)

Joan/Voices	Here am I Little jumping Joan When nobody's with me I'm not alone. (*She stops skipping.*)
Joan	I'm not alone.

She holds hands with her voices. A moment of strength and support.
Music ends. The Voices exit, taking the rope.
Joan is much steadier now, more in control.

Voice	Joan says nothing to her parents.
Voice	She speaks to no one.
Voice	She leaves the village and walks to a nearby town.
Uncle *(entering)*	To the home of her uncle.

Uncle wears a small white scarf tied round his neck.

Voice   The town is held by the Whites. But all around
    belongs to the Reds.

Uncle   I keep a scarf handy. Just in case.

Reveals a red scarf in his pocket. He eyes Joan wearily. The
conversation has been going on for some time.

Joan	I'm not moving till you agree.
Uncle	Do your mother and father know you're here?

Joan's face betrays her.

Uncle   Come on. I'll take you home. *(Tries to lead her
   off.)*

Joan   I told you – I'm not moving.

Uncle   Joan. You're a young girl. Your head's full of
   romantic nonsense. All this about saving France...

Joan   I'll stand here all day if I have to.

Uncle *(despairing)* Supposing I did take you ... Think what they'd say!
   All this flag-waving – you mustn't let yourself be taken in. White,
   red, blue – it makes no difference, they're all the same. War's a
   game to people like that – a chance to get rich. It doesn't matter
   which side wins, we're the ones who suffer, we're the ones who pay
   for it all.

Joan   I'm not moving.

Uncle *(impatient)* The Captain of the Guard is a busy man! He's got
   the whole town to protect!

Joan   If you won't take me then at least tell me where I
   can find him.

Uncle   They'll think you're mad ... You *are* mad! I'll go
   and fetch your father *(starts to go)*.

Joan   Then I'll go on my own. (*Uncle gives up in
   despair.)*

Uncle *(to the audience)* See what I'm up against? It's been going on for
   hours. People are beginning to stare. So in the end I take her
   (*They walk upstage, stop and return.)* And what happens? ... They
   think she's barking.

Joan   We'll go again tomorrow.

Uncle   What?

Joan   I'll tell them I've been sent by God – then they'll
   have to listen.

Uncle is speechless. They repeat the journey.

Uncle   This time they're convinced she's barking. We go again. And again. Every day for a whole week. Believe me when that girl gets something into her –

Joan   I never said it would be easy.

She drags him off again. They repeat the journey.

Uncle   I don't believe it. They're not laughing any more. They dread her coming. Everybody in town's talking about her. Crowds turn up everyday to see if they'll let her in. Not that she rants and raves or anything. Stands there, cool as a breeze, and says –

Joan   My name is Joan and I've been sent by God to save France.

Uncle   The crowd all shout and cheer ... The guard on the gate doesn't know where to put himself.

The Captain of the Guard enters (wearing white), accompanied by a White Soldier.

Captain   Eventually the Captain of the Guard agrees to see her.

Uncle   Thank God for that. (*He beats a welcome retreat.*)

Captain   So you're the girl who's been sent to save France?

Joan   I'm doing what the angels told me.

Captain   Angels? (*He shares a knowing look with the soldier.*) And they've sent you to drive out the English, have they?

Joan   I've been told I must go to the Prince of the Whites and tell him to put me in charge of his army.

Captain   Oh right. I understand... You're to be our new

Commander. In that case we should have the English beaten before the end of the week. (*They share a laugh.*) You're sure the angels wouldn't prefer the army to be commanded by a man?

Joan   I think they'd prefer to have it commanded by whoever can do it best. (*The laughter stops.*)

Captain (*irritated*) You think defending this town is easy, do you?

Joan   I should imagine it's very difficult.

Captain   And not made easier by having to waste time listening to the daydreams of young girls. (*Turns to go.*)

Joan   I'd like an escort of soldiers please, to take me to the court of the Prince.

Captain   Will you listen to her?! Soldiers now. How many? Any particular kind? Archers? Cavalry? We've dozens just idling around. After all, it's only a war!

Joan   I'd also like a horse... And some men's clothes. If commanding the army can only be done by a man, then perhaps I ought to start dressing like one.

Captain   .What you need is a boot up the backside! (*White Soldier restrains him.*)

White Soldier   People are talking. Some say she's the girl in the prophecy.

Captain   Prophecy? The girl's a lunatic. She wants throwing off the roof!

White Soldier   Why not give her what she wants?

Captain   Oh sure! Why not? Let her run the whole show!

White Soldier   We've troubles enough ... Send her to the Prince. Chances are she'll be caught by the English before she's half way there. And if not ... let the Prince throw her off the roof.

The Captain thinks it over. They both exit. Music in.
Voices appear carrying a set of men's clothes.

Voice	You see. You *can* do it. You *can* make them listen.

Joan's doubts return immediately.

Joan	I can't keep it up. This is not me. It's like being in a dream.

Voice (*removing the white cloth round Joan's waist*) The war isn't a dream. Only you can end it. (*Voices offer Joan the men's clothes.*)

Joan	Will wearing these make them listen?

Voice	You're as good as any man.

They help her into the men's clothes.

Joan	This is madness. It's a week's journey to the Prince's court. I've never been beyond the village. What will my mother and father say?

Voice	Trust in your voices.

Joan	What if I get caught? The English are every-where – they'll be watching every road.

Voice	You are not alone.

Joan	I'm sorry, I can't do this. You're going to have to find someone else!

Voice (*insistent*)	There *is* no one else.

Voices exit leaving Joan in the men's clothes. Music ends.
Joan repositions.

Joan	We travel at night – silently, our horses' hooves wrapped with rags. Enemy soldiers are everywhere. We pass their camps like shadows. The soldiers with me are kind. They take care

of me. They keep me safe. When the sun comes up we sleep –
sometimes hidden in the woods – sometimes in the home of a
villager.

*Joan lays down to sleep. A peasant woman enters. She wears neutral
colours. She places a blanket over Joan and sits nearby.*

Peasant Woman   I knew 'twas her alright. Young girl in men's
clothes. We'd heard whispers o'course. Rumours swarm like bees in
desperate times. The Reds heard 'em too. If you ask me, her has 'em
good and rattled. They be searching everywhere.

Two Red soldiers enter.

Peasant Woman   Come in, lads! Look where you wants – turn the
place upside down – I don't want nobody saying I be harbouring
fugitives!

*The two soldiers look around. They see the blanketed figure lying on
the floor and move towards it. They are about to lift the blanket.*

Peasant Woman   And don't you be worrying about my old man
there. You won't wake him – he been dead these last five year!

*The soldiers are stopped in their tracks. They give eachother a glance
and beat a hasty retreat. The peasant woman enjoys a good laugh.
Joan wakes up and hands the blanket back.*

Joan   Thank you for your kindness ... And your courage.

She exits.

Peasant Woman   There be something about that girl. You feels it in your bones. If you ask me, it be true. Her has been sent by God.

Music link as peasant woman exits. The Prince and the Duke enter. Both wear white. The Prince has a small white crown.

Prince   What do you mean he won't accept credit? Who does he think he is? I'm the king, at least I should be, at any rate I'm the Prince! And who is he? Some miserable shoemaker! Tell him he has no choice. Tell him if the Prince needs shoes it's a shoemaker's duty to provide them! I mean take a look! See   holes! What sort of Prince walks round with holes in his shoes?!

Duke   I think the problem is you didn't pay him for the last pair – or the pair before that.

Prince   So I haven't paid him. So what? Do I have to do everything around here myself? Do I have to attend to every last pifling detail – what's the point of having servants?

Duke   You haven't paid them either.

Prince   Well, what's the point of a having a state treasury!

Duke   There's nothing in the state treasury.

Prince   Well, why not?! Where's the money? Who's spent it? It wasn't me! It definitely wasn't me!

Duke   It's been spent on the war. Armies are expensive – especially armies that lose.

Prince   Then it's not my fault, is it? It shouldn't be me who has to suffer. You're the Duke – you're supposed to sort things out. Raise more money. What do people expect me to do –   walk round with holes in my shoes? Put up the taxes!

Duke   There's nothing left to tax.

Prince   What do you mean there's nothing left to tax? You can't have taxed everything! What about shoes? Have you taxed shoes?

Duke   Several times.

Prince   Alright then – what about hats? Tax everyone who wears a hat!

Duke   We've done that too.

Prince   Well, there must be something you haven't taxed! What about words? Have you taxed words?

Duke   Words?

Prince   Words! A gold coin for every word spoken. That should fill the treasury – all the gossip there is about this Joan whatever-her-name-is. Who is she anyway? And what's this Captain doing sending me his village idiots? Why can't he deal with her himself? I'm the Prince – the King by rights – and who is she? Some half-wit farm girl who thinks she's seen angels. Send her packing! Tell her to go and feed the pigs!

Duke   People are saying she's the girl in the prophecy.

Prince   What prophecy? What are you talking about? I've never heard of any prophecy!

Duke   It's moonshine – some old wives tale about a village maid sent by God to save France. All the same, the girl could be of use to us. People are desperate, ready to believe anything. They're beginning to listen to what she says.

Prince   Then they must be mad!

Duke   She says you're the true and rightful King of France.

Prince   What?

Duke   We're losing this war. Our soldiers are deserting in droves. If the English attack now, we're finished. So if this 'half-wit farm girl' can lift people's spirits with her superstitious fairy-tales, then it will certainly do us no harm!

Prince   In that case, do as you must. But deal with her yourself, I'll have no muddy-booted milk maid trudging over my floors.

Duke	She insists on speaking to the Prince.
Prince	Well, she can't!
Duke	In person.
Prince	Then you be the Prince. *(puts the crown on the Duke's head)* There! It's what you've always wanted, isn't it? You be the Prince – you speak to her!

Music in as they exit. Joan and her Voices enter. The Voices spruce Joan up ready to see the Prince. She's nervous and panicky. Music underscores.

Joan	What if he refuses to see me? What if I've come all this way for nothing.
Voice	Remember the Captain of the Guard? Believe in yourself.
Joan	But this is different. This is the royal court. There'll be Lords and Ladies, all in fine clothes.
Voice	And under the finery, flesh and blood – no different to yours.
Joan	But they don't talk like me. They have smooth accents – they use long words.
Voice	Long words and smooth accents won't drive out the English.
Joan	What if they won't listen? What if they all laugh at me?
Voice	Speak with the Prince. Only the Prince.
Joan	But what will I say? I don't know how you speak to a prince.
Voice	Tell him he is the true and rightful king of France.
Joan	How will I recognise him? I've never seen him before – I don't even know what he looks like!

Voice   Stay calm ... and use your wits.

Voices exit. Joan summons up her courage.

Joan   I'm walking through the streets. People are
waving. Crowds, smiling, calling out my name. Women lean from
windows. Boys stand on rooftops. They're throwing flowers. They're
cheering me on. I reach the castle. The gates open. I can see the
great hall with its pointed rooves and arched windows. I climb some
steps. A corridor, dark and cool, my boots ring like church bells.
Huge wooden doors swing back. And I stand in a blaze of light.
(Music ends. She rubs her eyes, half-blinded. Gazes upwards.)
Carved faces leer down from the rafters. *(She begins to regain her
focus. She looks straight out at the audience.)* A thousand eyes stare
at me. Silk dresses, ermin gowns. No one speaks.

*The Prince and the Duke appear, peering at Joan from a distance. The
Duke is wearing the Prince's crown.*

Prince   Is that her? The girl's a lunatic alright – she
doesn't even know whether she's a man or a woman. Well, go on,
what are you waiting for?

The Duke approaches Joan.

Duke   Welcome to our court. We heard the crowds.
You're obviously very popular.

Joan   The people are kind.

Duke   It seems they believe you're the girl in the
prophecy – that you've been sent by God.

Joan   The angels told me I must speak to the Prince.

Duke   And what did they tell you to say?

Joan *(wary)*   They told me to speak to the Prince. Only with the
     Prince.

Duke   And who do you think you're speaking with now?

Joan   I don't know. I'm not sure.

The Prince roars with laughter.

Prince *(applauding)* But not the Prince! And never will be! Well done,
young woman! Royalty is in the blood. Even a farm girl can tell.
*(Takes the crown from the Duke's head and replaces it on his own.
To Joan)* Your Prince greets you.

Joan   You are not the Prince.

Prince   What!

The Duke enjoys a laugh.

Prince   What do you mean, I'm not the Prince? Who do
you think I am? Of course, I'm the Prince! Ask anyone – I'm the
Prince of the Whites!

Duke   Even a farm girl can tell.

Prince   The girl's an idiot – throw her out!

The Duke takes Joan's arm.

Joan   You are the King. You are the true and rightful
King of France. *(Pause. They are speechless.)*

Prince   The King? *(gathering himself together)* Yes ... yes,
you're right ... She's right. I'm the king. I'm not the Prince, I'm the
King. She's absolutely right. I'm the true and rightful King of
France!

Joan	Give me your crown.
Prince	I beg your pardon?
Joan	Give me your prince's crown.
Duke	Your majesty –

Prince *(taking it from his head)* What do want with my crown?

Joan   Swear that in giving me this crown, you hand over to me your entire kingdom and everything in it.

Duke   This has gone far enough.

Prince   Wait! *(intrigued)* You're asking me to give you my entire kingdom?

Joan   All your wealth and everything you possess.

Prince   To a farm girl, from some village in the country?

Joan   To a maid who has been sent by God.

Duke   Don't listen to her.

Prince   What if she's telling the truth? What if she *has* been sent by God?

Duke   It's nonsense – she's been sent by no one!

Prince   Then how did she know who I was? How did she know I was the Prince?

Duke   You told her!

Prince   No! No, she *knew!*

Joan   Give me your crown.

Pause. The Prince considers hard. He is completely entranced by Joan.

Duke   Don't do it!

The Prince makes a decision.

Prince *(handing the crown to Joan)* In handing over this crown, I give to you my entire kingdom and everything in it ... Let all in my court bear witness.

Joan   You are the poorest man in France. A man who owns nothing. Kneel.

Prince   I beg your pardon.

Joan   Kneel down.

Duke   This is lunacy.

The Prince kneels at Joan's feet.

Joan   God has chosen you, the poorest man on earth, to be the true and rightful King of France.

She places the crown back on his head. The Prince rises to his feet, absolutely elated.

Prince   Did you hear? Did you all hear? The true and rightful King, chosen by God! Isn't that what I've always said? Isn't that what I've been telling you all? Not some common-or-garden Prince. I'm the King – the King of France – chosen by God!

Duke   I suspect the English may not quite see it that way.

Joan   I shall drive out the English.

Duke   Oh in that case we've nothing to worry about. They must be quaking in their boots.

Joan *(to the Prince)* The angels said you must put me in command of your army.

Prince   Then the angels must be obeyed.

Duke   This is like a nightmare!

Prince　　　　　　　What do you want me to do – disobey God? *(to Joan, his excitement rising)* You shall be my Commander in Chief. I'll tell the whole army to do what you say. You'll have five thousand soldiers ... ten thousand ... fifty thousand!

Duke　　　　　　　We don't even have five hundred! The army's lost virtually every battle it's fought. There's hardly any of it left!

Prince　　　　　　Then get another! Do I have to do everything around here myself? You're the Duke – you're supposed to sort things out! The girl wants an army – so go away and find her one!

The Duke exits in a rage. The Prince calms immediately. His tone with Joan is intense, almost reverential.

Prince　　　　　　Is it true? Do you really talk with angels?

Joan　　　　　　　They're my voices.

Prince　　　　　　Was it them told you I was the Prince? How did you know it wasn't the Duke? Was it the angels? Did they tell you?

Joan　　　　　　　I don't know – I –

Prince　　　　　　It was, wasn't it? They whispered in your ear, they told you I was the true and rightful King. *(Beat)* The Duke doesn't believe you, you know. He thinks the prophecy is just a fairytale. He thinks you're mad.

Joan　　　　　　　Sometimes I think I must be.

Prince　　　　　　No. You're not mad. You're the most true and honest person I've ever met. You're God's holy messenger. He's chosen you to drive out the English. Just like the prophecy. He's sent you to make me the true and rightful King of France!

Music in as Prince exits. Joan remains. Voices enter with a white and gold banner. Joan runs up to them.

Joan *(elated)* I did it! I did what you said! I used my wits – and it worked. The Prince listened to me – just like you said – he believed in me! *(Beat)* The Duke didn't though. He tried to trick me. He thinks I'm mad. But not the Prince – the Prince believes. He believes God has chosen me to drive out the English!

Voice *(offering her the banner)* So now that is what you must do.

Joan's euphoria evaporates immediately.

Voice　　　　　　　Lead the army of the Whites.

Fears and doubts return. Joan draws back from the banner.

Joan　　　　　　　I don't know anything about armies.

Voice　　　　　　　Soldiers need courage. You must show them how to overcome their fear.

Joan　　　　　　　A real battle? Fighting?

Voice　　　　　　　There will be suffering. Many will die.

Joan　　　　　　　Isn't there some other way?

Voice　　　　　　　You know there isn't.

Joan　　　　　　　There must be. I don't want this. Not killing people!

Voice　　　　　　　Take the banner.

Joan hesitates, then takes it.

Joan　　　　　　　You won't leave me? You'll stay close?!

The Voices help Joan raise the banner.

They exit as the English Soldier and English Commander enter. Music ends. The English Commander and English Soldier wear blue. The English Soldier carries a bow.

Commander   Left. Left. Left right left ... Soldiers – Halt! Take up your positions.

The soldier takes up position and starts to string his bow. He speaks to the audience as he works.

English Soldier   We know she's on her way – the Whites haven't tried to hide it. Every soldier in the line's on about her. A miraculous maid sent to drive us into the sea.

Commander *(to the soldier)* It's a scare story. They lose half their army, so they invent a load of drivel to try and put the wind up you. It's the oldest trick in the book.

English Soldier *(to the audience)* Trick or not, she's managed to put life into what's left of their soldiers. They were all set to surrender till they heard she were coming. Then this massive cheer went up. You could hear it for miles.

Commander   They don't stand a chance. What difference can a slip of a girl make?!

The Soldier tests his bow.

English Soldier *(to the audience)* Commander's right. The Commander's always right. So how come I have these rats gnawing away inside my gut?

Joan appears. She forms an image – her white and gold standard raised.

English Soldier   Then we see her. Straight in front of us. Not a soldier with her. What's she think she's doing? (*He levels his bow.*) She's only a lass. She's in range. We could kill her where she stands.

Joan (*out to the audience*) English soldiers! I wish you no harm. I come to speak to you in peace!

English Soldier (*quietly to himself*) Go away, will you. Get out the way.

Joan   If you'd come to our country as friends, we would have made you welcome. We'd have asked you into our homes, given you food and drink, treated you as guests. But you came as enemies. You came to kill us, to burn our houses and steal our land. (*Beat*) I don't want to fight you. I hate this war. Leave now and not a finger will be raised against you. Not one of you will be harmed. But if you stay, then we'll fight – just as you would if your homes were in danger. Remember your families, those praying for your safety, and go. Go now. Leave our country.

English Soldier (*his bow still levelled*) There's this long silence. Nobody moves – not a soldier. Maybe it's the thought of our own families – or just the simple way she talks – but somehow she's got to us.

Commander   Shoot her! ... What are you waiting for? Shoot her down!

English Soldier   Nobody moves.

Commander   What's the matter with you all! I'm giving you an order! Shoot the girl down!

English Soldier   She can hear him alright. Hears every word. She doesn't even flinch. Just stands there. Like she's no fear.

Commander   She's got you bewitched! Kill her!! (*He finally grabs the Soldier's bow and aims.*)

English Soldier   The Commander fires an arrow. We watch it flash towards her. We hear it thud into her chest.

Joan staggers. The banner falls to the ground. She disappears from sight.

English Soldier   Nobody makes a sound. It's like we're all frozen. Somehow it can't be that easy, it can't be over with that quick. And at the same time this dreadful ache starts tearing away at us, like we've shot down one of our own.

Commander   So much for the miraculous maid. So much for being sent by God. One shot – that's all it took – one well-aimed dart!

English Soldier   Maybe he's right. Maybe it was just a scare-story. Maybe she got us rattled over nothing.

Commander   She was a witch! She cast a spell on you all!

English Soldier   Some soldier down the line starts to cheer. Then another. And another. Till we're all at it. The whole battalion. Dancing and whooping like maniacs!

The Commander and the Soldier dance around with eachother, shouting and chanting. Percussion in – low and threatening. The soldiers hear it. Their chanting stops. Percussion builds. Commander and Soldier share an anxious glance.

English Soldier   What is it? What's going on?

Percussion becomes deafening. Commander and soldier become very frightened.

Commander   The Whites ...! It's the Whites!

English Soldier   We look across the field. It's their soldiers – hurtling towards us – eye's burning – screaming and roaring like some wild raging fire!

Joan appears again, waving her banner.

English Soldier *(backing away)* And then we see her. Right at the front – her white banner reaching to heaven – like no arrow ever touched her!

Commander　　　It's the devil. It's Satan rising out of hell! *(He makes a run for it.)*

English Soldier　　　Commander ... Commander!

Commander exits. The soldier grabs a weapon and starts to fight imaginary soldiers who beat him back.

English Soldier　　　We stand our ground! We fight like soldiers!... It's useless! We're tossed aside! Leaves in a storm!

His weapon goes flying. He scrambles to a place of safety on the set. Joan maintains her position. Percussion pulls back slightly.

English Soldier　　　I see the Commander. He's trying to reach the river. She's riding after him. He dives in – he's swimming across! He's trying to get away! She watches him. She could kill him, she could shoot him but she doesn't, she just watches. Then suddenly this eddy, this whirling pool of water, grabs him, pulls him into the current.

Joan throws out a rope.

Joan　　　Take it! Grab the rope!

English Soldier　　　She's trying to save him.

Joan　　　Take hold! Take the rope!

English Soldier   He stretches out. He tries to reach... Then nothing ... no sign, he just vanishes.

Joan sadly hauls in the rope.

English Soldier   I tell you there's something about that girl. Something nobody can explain.

English Soldier exits. Joan remains on stage. Percussion fades out. Music in to underscore. Voices enter. Joan is horrified by the scene of battle around her.

Joan   Blood. Torn flesh. Bulging eyes. Bodies broken and burnt. Is this what war is? Is this what God sent me to do?

Voices gently take the banner from her.

Joan *(feeling pain from a wounded shoulder)* Was it you who saved me?

Voice   It was your own belief. Your own will.

Joan   It's over now though, isn't it? It's all finished – I can go home.

The Voices don't agree.

Joan *(protesting)*   I've done what you told me. I've driven out the English.

Voice   You won a battle. The English are still here. Still in France.

Joan   You mean I'll have to go through all this again? Perhaps they'll go. Perhaps they'll just give up and leave.

Voice   You must take the Prince to Rheims.

Joan   Rheims?

Voice   Only when he's crowned in the Cathedral at
Rheims will he be recognised as the true and rightful King of France.

*She holds out the banner. Joan reluctantly takes it. Voices exit. Music
ends. The Prince and the Duke enter.*

Prince   Didn't I say? Didn't I tell you? She's been sent by
God. I knew it the moment I set eyes on her, that girl will save
France!

Prince   Order a banquet! Food, wine, musicians – the
biggest celebration the court has seen – with Joan as guest of
honour!

Joan   Your majesty, there's no time to celebrate. We
have to leave.

Prince   Leave? What for? Whyever should we leave?

Joan   I have to take you to Rheims – where all true
Kings of France are crowned.

Prince   Now? Straight away?

Duke   Joan clearly doesn't realise that Rheims is five
hundred miles away and that the entire English army stands in our
way.

Prince   Haven't you been listening? Joan's beaten the
English. She sent them packing!

Duke   We defeated one small section of the English
army, a few hundred soldiers who were taken by surprise. We're not
likely to be so lucky a second time.

Joan   Luck had nothing to do with it. Men gave their
lives to make you King.

Duke   Your majesty, if by some miracle, we were ever
to get as far as Rheims, you'd find it held by the army of the Reds.

You could lose everything, even your life.

Prince *(worried)*   Is this true?

Joan   My voices have told me we must go.

Prince *(reassured)* There you are. The angels have spoken. We shall do as God commands!

Prince exits, followed by the Duke. Music in to underscore.
Joan repositions. She's now feeling confident and exuberant.

Joan   This time no rags muffle our horses' hooves. We ride with banners raised and trumpets sounding. This time our enemies know we're here!

Music swells. She parades in triumph, waving her banner.

Joan   News of our journey spreads like fire. Men run to join us. Swords, lances, axes, bows. My army doubles and doubles again. Rank after rank. Pennants flutter in the breeze. Men in their thousands– laughing, cheering, shouting, urging us forward!

Music stops. Two soldiers appear (one red, one blue). They form an image, holding red and blue banners.

Joan   Then we see them. Lined up. Waiting for us. The steel of their weapons glinting in the sun.

Joan raises her banner.

Joan   For France and for Freedom!

Immediate percussion. Joan and the two soldiers rush at each other, weaving chaotic whirling patterns with their banners. A fierce and frantic battle. Eventually, the percussion begins to calm, the battle slows. The blue and red banners droop to the ground. The two soldiers retreat. Joan lifts her banner high.

Joan   The day is ours!

Percussion continues. Joan's mood is now one of triumph and celebration.

Joan   No one dares stand in our way now. At every town, people open their gates and welcome us in. Red and blue flags are torn down. White ones hoisted in their place. People invite me into their houses. Give me food. Sing songs for us. Children hang flowers around my neck. Women run to touch my feet. It feels like the whole of France is set ablaze! *(Beat)* Then at last, we arrive at Rheims.

A Red Soldier appears and forms an image. He levels his banner at Joan. Joan responds. They confront each other as if about to do battle. At the last moment, the Red Soldier loses his courage, puts down his banner as a sign of surrender. The Prince enters.

Prince *(jubilant)* Didn't I tell you? Didn't I always say? The true and rightful King of France!

He picks up the Red banner and tosses it offstage.

Joan   Church bells ring as we enter the city. We parade through the streets like conquering heroes – to the doors of the cathedral itself!

Music – a fanfare. Joan and the Prince reposition. The Duke enters carrying an extravagantly decorated crown. He positions himself ready to perform the ceremony, but the Prince takes the crown from him and hands it to Joan. He kneels at Joan's feet. The Duke is furious.

Joan   I pronounce you the true and rightful King of France.

Music swells. The Prince exits in procession followed by the Duke. Music ends. Joan's uncle appears in the background. Joan is now triumphant – no trace of the hesitant little girl we saw at the beginning.

Joan   Uncle? Uncle is it you? It's good to see you! *(She welcomes him warmly.)* Did you come for the coronation? Did you see me place the crown on the Prince's head? Wasn't it wonderful – wasn't it magnificent! You didn't believe me, did you? You didn't think I could do it. I defeated the English, Uncle, – me, little jumping Joan. I brought the Prince to Rheims and I made him King – the true King of France! *(noticing his expression)* What's the matter? Aren't you pleased?

Uncle   I'm pleased the war's over.

Joan   But it isn't. It's not over yet. The English are still in France.

Uncle   In Normandy. One small part of France.

Joan   One part is too much. This is our country not theirs.

Uncle   Joan, I've come to take you home.

Joan   Home?

Uncle   Your family – your mother and father. You haven't even been in touch. *(For once Joan has no quick answer.)* You don't belong here … Not with people like these.

Joan   People like what? I can't come home. Not now. I have to win the war. I have to fight for the King.

Uncle   Let the king fight his own wars ... Maybe then there wouldn't be as many.

Joan   What do you mean?

Uncle   Joan, open your eyes. These people don't care about you. They care about themselves ... about money, about living the sort of life you and I can only dream about.

Joan   He's the King. He was chosen by God.

Uncle   They've all been chosen by God – every king and ruler known to man. How do you think they get people to die for them?

Joan *(getting agitated)* It's not true. You're telling lies. The King has been chosen by God – the angels told me!

Uncle *(treading carefully)* These voices you hear ... maybe they're something else ... maybe they're not angels at all.

Joan   What do you mean? How can you say that?

Uncle   Did they tell you they were angels?

Joan   Who do you think they are? Who else could they be?!

Uncle   I don't know. Maybe we all hear voices, maybe they're inside us somewhere ... part of ourselves.

Joan   That's ridiculous. I've never heard anything so stupid! They're angels – they speak to me – only to me! They bring me God's holy message!

Uncle   You've done enough here. More than enough. More than anyone could have dreamed. Come home. Come back to the village ... It's where you belong.

Joan *(aloof, back in control)* You're the one who belongs in the village. You go. I have more important things to do.

She exits. Uncle watches her leave, then exits.
Lights up on the Prince and a shoemaker – the Prince is trying on new
shoes. The Duke looks on.

Prince   They pinch my toes ... They pinch my toes I tell
you! I'm the King, crowned and annointed, a King shouldn't be
expected to wear shoes that pinch his toes. Take them off! Take
them off!

The Shoemaker helps him off with the shoes.

Duke   It isn't just my opinion. Your entire court thinks
so. Joan's plan is reckless. It's foolhardy.

Prince   I don't think it's reckless and foolhardy. The King
of England deserves to be driven into the sea. Serves him right – he
should never have come here in the first place. France belongs to me
not to him. *(Pause)* These are just as bad! What kind of shoemaker
are you? Are these the best you've got?!

The Shoemaker helps him with another pair.

Duke   The English want peace – the Reds too. They're
ready to make a deal with us.

Prince   What deal? There's no deal to be had. I'm the
King and that's all there is to it. They'll just have to get used to it ...
You call these white? I've never seen a more pinky-looking white in
all my life. You wouldn't be trying to make fun of me, would you?

The Shoemaker helps him take them off.

Duke   They're willing to accept you as King ... We might
have to let them keep Normandy in return, but we'd still control
most of France.

Shoemaker shows the Prince another pair.

Prince   Straps! I hate straps! No decent pair of shoes
should ever have straps!

And another pair.

Duke   Don't you see? We're in a position of strength. It's
us calling the tune now.

Prince   They never wanted to talk about deals when they
were winning!

Duke   We can't go on fighting forever. People are tired of
it – on both sides.

Prince   Joan's not. She's not tired of it. She thinks we
should attack. She says we should drive the English into the sea.

Duke   What for? They want peace. They want a
compromise. All we have to do is sit down and talk.

Prince   You're forcing them! Shoes should never be
forced!

Duke   We have a real chance to end this war, to get the
country back to normal. It would save lives ... save money.

Prince   Money?

Duke   War costs money – lots of money – money that
could be spent on other things *(indicates the shoes)*.

The Shoemaker shows the Prince the final pair.

Prince *(interested)* Now these look something like.

Duke   Then you agree?

Prince   Alright, you've made your point. I don't know why you bother me with all this triviality anyway – you're the Duke, you're supposed to handle all that kind of stuff. Talk to Joan, sort it out with her.

The Duke takes the shoes and gently slips them onto the Prince's foot. The Prince parades around, admiring himself.

Prince   I think I like them ... I do. I like them.

The Prince exits. The Duke remains, much pleased with himself. Joan enters.

Joan *(frosty)*   Where's the King?

Duke *(tidying up the shoes)* The King is busy.

Joan   I have to speak to him.

Duke   He's not to be disturbed.

Joan   What are you doing? Let me past!

Duke   His instructions were that you should talk with me.

Joan   You?

Duke   On all matters.

Joan *(reluctantly concedes defeat.)* We're wasting time. While we're holding parties and banquets, the English are bringing up reinforcements. We have to attack them now before they get any stronger.

Duke	That's impossible.
Joan	Tell the king I shall be assembling the army.
Duke	The army has been disbanded.
Joan	Disbanded?
Duke	The soldiers have been sent home.
Joan	On whose orders?
Duke	The King has agreed to open negotiations.

Joan I don't believe you. He wouldn't do that – the King would never trust the English!

Duke The English have declared a ceasefire. They've asked for peace talks.

Joan Only because they're losing! They're trying to buy time! The moment they're strong enough they'll attack. We have to drive them out, or France will never be safe!

Duke France will never be safe while it's army is led by a headstrong war-monger who's lost touch with reality.

Joan Tell the King I shall be leaving for Normandy to attack the English.

Duke Then you'll attack them alone... Perhaps your angels will help you.

The Duke exits. Joan remains. Music in to underscore. Voices enter. They stand watching Joan.

Joan *(fuming)* How dare he? How dare he talk to me like that?! *(Voices make no response.)* Who brought the Prince to Rheims? Who crowned him King? Not him! Not the Duke! Did you hear what he said to me?!

Voice It wasn't him I was listening to.

Joan What?

Voice	Emotion isn't enough.
Voice	You must also learn to think.
Joan	You're beginning to sound like my uncle!
Voice	Maybe you should have listened to him.

Joan   .... Not you? You're not turning against me now are you? It was you who told me what to do – God's orders, you said, you told me I had to save France!

Voice   And now you must decide how best to do it. Life isn't simple.

Voice   You're not a girl any more. You must try to think like an adult!

Joan   You told me I had to drive out the English.

No one else, you said. I left my home – my family – everything. Men have fought battles for me – given their lives – I can't betray them! What would people say? They didn't give their lives to make a deal with the English, they died to save France! *(Pause. Voices turn to go.)* Go then. Go away ... You think I need you? People are writing songs about me. They touch my clothes as I pass ... I'm the maid in the prophecy. The girl chosen by God!

Voices exit. Joan watches them go, then also exits. Music ends. A Gatekeeper enters (white). A Scribe comes up to him (neutral colours). She has poor eyesight.

Scribe   I'm obliged if you'd give me a bit of assistance, ma'am

Gatekeeper   I'm not a ma'am, I'm a sir.

Scribe *(taking a close look)* So you be.

Gatekeeper   What do you want?

Scribe   They say the Keeper of the Gate be enquiring after me but I be danged if I can find him. Most likely drinking himself daft on all the tolls he manages to fiddle eh?! *(laughs)*

Gatekeeper   I'm the Keeper of the Gate.

Scribe *(taking a closer look)* So you be –

Gatekeeper   Who are you?

Scribe   Gatekeeper needs a man o' letters, so they says. So here I be... 'Cept I not be a man.

Gatekeeper   You're a scribe?

Scribe   No finer hand in all of Normandy! *(Produces pen and paper.)* To a lady is it?

Gatekeeper   No it isn't.

Scribe*(with a twinkle in her eye)* I be a poet in affairs concerning the heart.

Gatekeeper   Write what I tell you. *(The scribe settles down.)* To the Court of the King ... Dear Duke ...

Scribe   Duke! Then this be a message of importance.

Gatekeeper   I received your letter about the girl, Joan.

Scribe   God bless her and love her. The girl's a diamond.

Gatekeeper   She arrived in Normandy a week ago and is staying in our town. She rides out every day to attack the English who are camped outside our walls.

Scribe   May the saints protect her.

Gatekeeper   However – the soldiers with her are too few to drive away the English and I agree with you that her actions can only damage the peace process.

Scribe   There be no creature in France wanting peace more than that young girl!

Gatekeeper   If you don't stop this interrupting I'll find myself another scribe! *(continuing, choosing his words carefully.)* She is always the last to return to the safety of our walls and is always hotly pursued by the enemy. Closing the gates would ensure her capture – or death.

Scribe *(stunned)* May God forgive you for such a thought.

Gatekeeper   I will of course treat this with the utmost secrecy, and I thank you for your generous gift.

Scribe   I'll write no more! This be the devil's work. No hand of mine will pen such evil!

She thrusts the letter back at the Gatekeeper. He grabs her wrist.

Gatekeeper   How many fingers do you have on this hand?

Scribe   As many as your own – though mine be clean!

Gatekeeper *(drawing a knife)* If one word of this reaches the wrong ears, you'll be left with neither clean nor dirty.

He releases her wrist and takes the letter. The Scribe quickly hides her hands behind her back. The Gatekeeper exits. The Scribe starts to go but walks into Joan coming in.

Joan   I'm sorry ... Did I startle you?

Scribe   Bless you girl, you startled the entire world. Be you going outside the walls?

Joan   Of course.

Scribe   Stay. Not this day. Don't go.

Joan   Why not?

Scribe   There be enemies. Enemies you never dreamed of ... I dares say no more.

Joan   I must do what God has commanded... But I thank you for your kindness. And your courage

Joan exits.

Scribe   Sometimes I be thankful for these bad eyes. This world has things best not seen.

Scribe exits. Percussion in to softly underscore. The English soldier enters.

English Soldier   I thought I'd seen the last of her after that first time. She could have slaughtered every one of us that day – we'd have done the same to them soon enough. She didn't even take prisoners, just let us all walk off. *(Beat)* Now here she is again – in some pokey little Normandy town – taking us on almost single-handed. What drives her? What keeps her going?

Percussion builds. Joan runs in as if chased by the enemy. The soldier watches as she tries to escape. She finds her exit blocked as if by a gate being shut.

Joan   Let me in! It's me – it's Joan! *(She runs to a different exit. Same result.)* Open the gate! Why don't you let me in?! *(She backs away into the soldier arms. She struggles for a moment then realises it's futile.)*

English Soldier   What I can't understand is her own side. Seems like they wanted us to capture her – wanted her locked away.

Percussion stops. The soldier releases her and exits. Pause. A silence. Joan suddenly feels very much alone and vulnerable. She's a captive. She looks round for her Voices.

Joan   Are you there? I can't hear you.

An English Noble (blue) and two Red Lawyers enter. They appear in a different space to Joan who continues trying to contact her Voices.

The two scenes are entirely separate but happen at the same time.

Red Lawyer 1   I don't know. What if she's not guilty?

English Noble   She hears voices. She claims they're from God. What more do you want?

Red Lawyer 2   She could be telling the truth. It has been known. People are sometimes visited by angels.

English Noble   What is it with you Reds? Do you want the other side to win?

Joan   Where are you? Why won't you come?

Red Lawyer 2   You're the ones who want to convict her – why don't *you* put her on trial?

English Noble   It has to be Frenchmen. People won't believe it otherwise.

Red Lawyer 1   They won't believe it anyway. She has a lot of support, even our among our own.

Red Lawyer 2   Some are even calling her a saint.

English Noble   That's exactly why you need to make them believe she's a witch!

Joan   I didn't mean what I said ... I'm sorry ... Come back.

English Noble   All you have to do is find her guilty. We'll do to the rest.

The English Noble moves into the background. Red Lawyer bangs a staff to open the trial. The two scenes come together. Joan struggles to pull herself together.

Red Lawyer 1   You are charged with witchcraft, blasphemy and treason against the Kingdom of France. How do you plead?

Joan   If I'm to be put on trial then I demand to be

judged by the true and rightful King of France. Not by foreign invaders and their French lackeys.

Red Lawyer 2   I advise you to show respect to your betters.

Joan   When I see them I will show respect.

Red Lawyer 2   You have a great deal of arrogance. Is it for that reason you stand before us in men's clothes?

Joan   The clothes I wear are my own business.

Red Lawyer 1   Perhaps they're to indicate that you consider yourself equal to a man.

Joan   They indicate whatever you wish.

Red Lawyer 2   So you believe it right that a woman should think of herself equal to a man?

Joan   Only in some things... In others she should think of herself as better.

Red Lawyer 1   I see. Tell me then ... do you accept the word of the Bible – that God created man in his own image?

Joan *(wary)* That is what we're taught.

Red Lawyer 1   From which it follows that God must be male. *(Joan hesitates, unsure of her ground.)* I'm asking you whether God is male or female.

Joan *(struggling for the right words)* I'm not sure what God is.

Red Lawyer 2   You're not sure what God is. But you claim to have heard his voice.

Joan   That's not true. I've never heard God's voice.

Red Lawyer 1   Then whose voice have you heard?

Joan   His angels – God's holy angels.

Red Lawyer 2   You know that for certain do you?

Joan   What are trying to say?

Red Lawyer 1   How do you know they're angels? Do they have wings?

Joan   Wings?

Red Lawyer 1   Wings. Do your angels have wings?

Joan *(struggling again)* I don't know ... I'm not sure ...

Red Lawyer 2   But you've seen them?

Joan   Yes – No – I can't explain. I feel them. I know
when they're near.

Red Lawyer 1   And you hear their voices?

Joan   They speak to me. They tell me what to do.

Red Lawyer 2   Are they the voices of men or women?

Joan *(annoyed and confused)* I don't know ... I don't know what they
are.

Red Lawyer 2   Did they tell you they were angels?

Joan   They are. They're angels. I know they are!

Red Lawyer 1   You just said you don't know what they are.

Joan   You're trying to confuse me – you're trying to put
words in my mouth!

Red Lawyer 1   I think you're making this up. It's all make-
believe. You can't even tell us whether the voices you hear are men
or women!

Joan   They're neither! They're angels I tell you. Angels!

Red Lawyer 2   What did they say to you? Did they tell you their
names? Did they tell you they'd come from God?

Joan   They told me I'd been chosen!

Red Lawyer 1   By God? But why you? Why should God choose
you?

Joan   I don't know ... Why do you keep asking me these
questions? I don't know!

Red Lawyer 1   Why not one of your friends? Your mother or
father? Your uncle? The Duke? The Prince? Of all the men and
women in France why should God choose you – a simple-minded

village girl who can neither read nor write?

Joan *(starting to panic)* I don't know, I tell you. The prophecy ... because of the prophecy!

Red Lawyer 2   The prophecy?

Joan   The girl in the prophecy ... The maid who saves France.

Red Lawyer 2*(sensing victory)* Oh I see. So that's who you are? That's why God has chosen you? You're the maid in the prophecy.

Red Lawyer 1   But the prophecy is a fairy tale. It's hocus pocus.

Red Lawyer 2   Superstitious nonsense spread by old wives and village idiots.

Red Lawyer 1   The stuff of spells and magic. Of witchcraft.

Red Lawyer 2   Nothing to do with the Church – nothing to do with God.

Joan starts to get desperate.

Joan *(to her Voices)* Help me! What shall I say? Tell me what I should say!

Red Lawyer 1   Who are you talking to? Are they here now? Are they speaking to you? Are they telling you how to answer?

Joan   I need your help! Please – come to me!

Red Lawyer 2   What are they saying? Are they telling you to lie? Are they telling you to put a curse on us all?

Joan   I can't hear you. Speak to me ... where are you?

Red Lawyer 1   Perhaps they're hiding. Over in the corner. Beneath the floorboards? Crouching in the shadows? Why don't they come? What are they frightened of?

Red Lawyer 2   Have they deserted you? Have they run away? Have they left you to face this on your own?

Joan   Please! I need you! Come to me!

Red Lawyer 1   If they were angels they would. They'd listen.
They'd hear you calling. They'd answer your cries. *(Beat)* But these
aren't angels, are they? These are not voices from heaven. It isn't
messages from God they bring you. These are demons. Vile and full
of filth. These are the voices of the Devil!

Joan   They're angels! Why don't you believe me?
They're angels!

Red Lawyer 2   Then where are they? Why can't you hear them?
Why do they refuse to help? Why have they abandoned you?!

Pause. Joan is completely defeated.

English Noble   She's said enough. Get it over with.

Music in to underscore. Red lawyers reposition.

Red Lawyer 2   You, the accused, have been found guilty of
witchcraft, blasphemy and countless crimes of evil. You are a
worthless and infamous girl who has brought dishonour to the name
of France and caused a false Prince to be crowned King.

Red Lawyer 1   This court sentences you to be taken from this
place to the place of execution, and burned as a witch.

Joan *(horrified)*   No. Not the fire!

Red Lawyer 2   In the name of justice and mercy, we offer you
one last chance to confess your sins and beg God's holy forgiveness.

Joan   What should I say? Speak to me ... what should I
say?!

Red Lawyer 1   Do you declare your voices to be those of the
Devil?

Joan	Is it true? Is that what you are?

Red Lawyer 2   Do you admit to using witchcraft to defeat the English in battle?

Joan	Why don't you answer me?!

Red Lawyer 1   Confess your sins to God. Or burn as the witch that you are.

Joan *(horrified)*	No ... Not burning ... Not the fire.
Red Lawyer 1	Confess and your life will be spared.

English Noble *(intervening quickly)* What are you saying? She's given her answer – she's guilty!

The English Noble starts to lead her off.

Joan   No! Wait! *(Terrified, she wrestles with the choice.)* I am what you say. I confess my sins and beg God's holy fogiveness.

Red Lawyer 2 *(not expecting this, thrown off guard)* You admit to using witchcraft?

Joan	I ... admit.
Red Lawyer 1	And your voices?
Joan	Demons ... They're the voice of the Devil.

Pause. The Red Lawyers realises they've blown it. The English Noble is furious.

English Noble	I blame you for this!
Red Lawyer 2	We did what you asked – we proved she's a witch!
English Noble	And spared her life!!

English Noble exits angrily. Red Lawyers scurry after him. Music link.
Joan stands alone. After a few moments the English Soldier enters
carrying a blue cloth. He holds it out to her.

English Soldier *(apologetic)* They say you have to wear this.

Joan   Am I not permitted a different colour?

English Soldier   I'm sorry.

Joan takes the blue cloth. Ties it around her waist. Looks down at
herself.

Joan   What will they do with me?

English Soldier   You're to be kept in prison. For life.

Joan   Here? In France?

English Soldier   In England... It's not as bad as you think. There
are good people in England. Ordinary men and women, like
yourself.

Pause. There is a closeness between them.

Joan   That day, that first battle ... do you believe I cast a
spell on you?

English Soldier   Not the kind of spell they mean.

Joan   What kind?

English Soldier   You have some sort of power ... Power to make
people believe they can do things – things they thought they never
could.

Joan   Does that mean I'm a witch?

English Soldier   Witches grow out of men's fear.

Joan   Then why?

English Soldier   Because you're different ... because you're strong.

Pause. For a moment there is a commonality between them then he breaks it and he exits. Joan is left alone. Music in to underscore.

Voices enter. Joan doesn't notice at first, then gradually becomes aware.

Joan   You're there aren't you? I can feel you.
(The Voices make no reply.) Why didn't you come?
Why did you leave me? *(Still no reply.)*
They told me you were demons.
They said you were the voice of the Devil.
Why are you looking at me? *(Silence.)*
Say something. Why don't you speak? *(Silence.)*
I know what you're thinking. Say it. Go on, say it!
(Silence. Then accusing them.) You weren't there.
You wouldn't speak to me. I didn't know what to do!
(They make no move, show no emotion.)
You told me to think like an adult. But I couldn't. I tried.
All I could think of was the fire. Burning into me. Scorching my
flesh! *(Pause.)* I was alone. I was frightened. *(They move up to her,
gently give her support.)* You are angels, aren't you?
I know you are.

*She pulls at the blue cloth around her waist. It falls to the floor.
Music ends. The English Soldier enters. He sees Joan but not her
Voices. He notices the blue cloth on the floor and picks it up.*

English Soldier   Don't do this.

Joan   It's alright. My voices are with me.

English Soldier   You know what they'll do to you.

Joan   I'm not afraid now.

English Soldier   Prison's not so bad. I've been there myself. You
 get used to it. At least you'd be alive! They might do some sort of
 deal – there's a peace process – you could be released – you might
 be out in a couple of years, free to go home!

Joan   You're a good man.

English Soldier *(pleading)* It's a piece of cloth. Just a piece of cloth.

He realises he's getting nowhere. He leaves.
Music in. The Voices start to turn the skipping rope and sing. Behind
them, if possible, a projection of flames.

Voices   Here am I
 Little Jumping Joan
 When nobody's with me
 I'm not alone.
 (They keep turning.)
 Here am I
 Little Jumping Joan
 When nobody's with me
 I'm not alone.

Joan jumps in and starts to skip. The skipping and singing get
stronger, building and developing into a joyful celebration.

Joan/Voices   Here am I
 Little Jumping Joan
 When nobody's with me
 I'm not alone
 Here am I
 Little Jumping Joan
 When nobody's with me
 I'm not alone

Here am I
Little Jumping Joan
When nobody's with me
I'm not alone.

The skipping stops. Projection of flames continues.
They hold the image.

Lights down.
The end.

OTHER PLAYS AND ADAPTATIONS BY NEIL DUFFIELD

2007	**Leopard**
2007	**A Christmas Carol**
2006	**Notre Dame de Paris**
2005	**The Emperor's New Clothes**
2004	**The Lost Warrior**
2003	**The Devil at Coventry**
2002	**The Emperor and the Nightingale**
2000	**The Firebird**
1999	**Skin and Bones**
1997	**Arabian Nights**
1997	**The Secret Garden**
1996	**Stripy Tales**
1995	**The Magic Story Bowl**
1993	**Dancing in my Dreams**
1992	**The Jungle Book**
1990	**The Ugly Duckling**
1989	**The Snow Queen**
1988	**Lilford Mill**

Details of these and others can be found
on the author's website.

http://homepage.ntlworld.com/n.duffield1